MW01128243

Mocha Latt

by

Sara Bourgeois

Chapter 1

Kari Sweet rummaged through her vanity on the hunt for her hairbrush. She wore a robe with one sock half on and a towel wrapped tightly around her head of long brown curls. Almost her entire wardrobe was splayed out across her bed, a symptom of her constant indecision on what she should wear.

As she rooted, she muttered under her breath—hold on, she knew where the darn thing was. Pausing for a moment, she shouted in the direction of her sister's room.

"Hey, Kasi? Kasi!"

No reply. Kari took this as an admission of guilt. She stomped across the hallway to her sister's bedroom, determined to right the injustice.

"Kasi, hey, you don't happen to have my hairbrush, do you?" she asked with a wide-eyed, innocent smile.

Kasi turned toward her sister as she finished sweeping the brush in question through her long straight brown hair.

"Oh, is this yours?" Kasi replied as though she had no idea she had her sister's favorite brush. "I just thought you wouldn't need it yet because, you know, it takes a long time for you to get ready."

To Kari, this was like waving a red cape in front a bull. Fuming, she grabbed the brush from her sister's hand and stomped back to her own bedroom. She didn't stop fuming until she was fully dressed.

She hated that her younger sister was right. Kari knew she had some serious issues when it comes to making decisions in the morning.

When Kari finally made it down to the kitchen, she realized she had just enough time to put on her makeup before they needed to get to their coffee shop and open it.

On Bitter Grounds had been operating for five years, ever since Kari and Kasi had taken over the lease after finishing college. Kari, the older sister, had her eye on the shop as soon as she had returned to their hometown of Mills Township after graduation.

Everything had worked out beautifully when Kasi graduated two years later, as they had signed the lease at almost exactly the same time.

"Finally. Come on, Kari, we need to get that roast on." Kasi handed her older sister fresh, hot coffee in a travel mug and hurried her out the door.

***

Kari fished about in the depths of her purse for the keys to the shop. The sisters had an hour before the shop's scheduled opening, just enough time to prepare for the day.

Not satisfied with simply giving the people of Mills Township an excellent cup of coffee to get them started, the girls wanted to fortify their customers with delicious pastries and breakfast items on their way to work.

They even decided to offer a tasty lunch option a few years back, and the idea had gone over well with their customers. The shop, along with their small-batch bean roasting strategy that served both the town and their national customers online, all took a lot of hard work and commitment—qualities the girls were blessed with in abundance.

Kari and Kasi's parents had always been upstanding members of the community and couldn't be prouder of the work ethic they had instilled in their beautiful daughters. The sisters had always worked hard in school and each received scholarships to prestigious universities.

Their years at college gave the sisters much-needed perspective as well as a solid education. Living outside Mills Township, they had seen first-hand what life was like in other towns and how different businesses affected the personality of the town. Strengthening their community was important to the Sweet family, and Kari and Kasi were proud to carry on the tradition.

As Kari fumbled with the door, Kasi started to think about the day ahead and the plans they had for the menu.

"What did we decide on for the special this week, Kari?" Kasi asked.

"I thought we decided on the mocha lattes and bagels with cream cheese, right?" Kari replied as she finally let her sister in through the door.

Kari and Kasi may have had their differences when it came to getting ready in the morning, but they were united in their passion for their business. Making decisions about which coffee and food they wanted to serve was very straightforward— the sisters always agreed almost instantly.

The Food and Retail Expo in Chicago they attended the month before had helped them take the business to the next level. The show was an amazing experience and had proven to be well worth their time.

They were initially reluctant to close shop for a whole week, but they had been amazed by the increase in web traffic since they'd been to the show and had made new connections.

The girls had always known that selling beans online would be the perfect complement to their brick-and-mortar shop, and the retail expo was just what they needed to kick it off. Upon their return, the On Bitter Grounds website practically had flames coming out of it, what with all the new orders coming in.

Perhaps the nicest part of the expo had been making friends with two great girls from another small town further up North along the coast.

Kari and Kasi hit it off immediately with Jenna Miller and Laura Newcomb, both small business owners in a town called Chesapeake Pointe. The four young women seemed to just get each other.

Maybe it was because they all came from similar backgrounds and knew everything there was to know about running a small-town business after years away. In fact, the girls had all hit it off so well that Jenna had made Kari and Kasi promise to visit Chesapeake Point soon—something they all knew meant they had made lifelong friends.

Jenna and Laura not only ran successful small businesses, but they'd also made quite a reputation for themselves by helping the local police department solve crimes. They told the sisters stories of catching murderers that were both exciting and a little scary.

Kari couldn't imagine being caught up in anything like that as Mills Township was way too quiet and sleepy for that sort of thing. Still, Jenna and Laura's stories brought both excitement and inspiration to the Sweet sisters.

If Jenna's bakery and Laura's candle store could be such successes, Kari and Kasi knew they could do the same thing with their coffee shop.

On the shop floor, Kari put the finishing touches on the day's blackboard list of specials they had decided on. She couldn't help but think about one particular customer who would especially enjoy what they had planned for the day.

The customer happened to be very handsome and a big fan of the On Bitter Grounds cream cheese bagel, which was made from a special recipe the girls had come up with a few months before.

This very special customer, Hunter Houston, was six-foot-two of pure ruggedness and has always served as the highlight of Kari's day.

Kari couldn't help but smile as she thought about Hunter and how much he'd enjoy their weekly special. Hunter was just so gorgeous she couldn't seem to get him off her mind.

She'd been thinking about Hunter coming in since she'd woken up, one of the reasons she'd agonized so much about looking perfect when she'd been getting ready that morning.

It looked like today could turn out to be another interesting day in Mills Township. Who said small towns were boring anyway?

Chapter 2

Hunter

Come on, Hunter, you can do better than this.

Hunter Houston liked nothing better than beginning each day with a five-mile-run. Today, however, he was a little slower on his overall time.

Despite having an iPod loaded with his favorite running songs, he still struggled with inner frustrations. His morning stretches that were meant to help loosen him up before his run didn't even seem to help with his tension today.

Pick up the pace, man, you have places to be and things to get done.

He had no problem waking this morning. He was usually already awake by the time the alarm clock goes off, but when he woke up today, he felt a little extra stressed. Running usually helped clear his mind and even helped him to pick up on clues he missed before but were somehow hiding at the back of his mind.

I have to tell Jo that we need to revisit that lead from last week. We missed something there.

Stopping on the porch, Hunter did his usual post-run stretches while drinking the last of his water. He pushed his hair off his forehead, wincing at the sweat now cooling on his skin.

He felt better already, but he knew the real endorphin rush wouldn't kick in until he was done and out of the shower. That's when the early start would really prove its worth. He'd been busy working a frustrating case that just wasn't budging, a real humdinger.

He might just have found a little chink of light in which to begin though—thanks to the run.

Not my best, but it will have to do. I'll get a quick shower and get ready for work.

He took the stairs two at a time and hurried through his morning routine and pulled on his uniform. He stood facing the full-length mirror in his bedroom and checked out his appearance.

He was tall, lean, and very fit. He prided himself on being in great shape for his own well-being—and so that he can be the best police officer he could. He never knew when he'd be called upon to chase down a crook or help someone out of a tight spot.

Standing at six-feet-two, with a mess of sandy blonde hair and piercing blue eyes, Hunter was pleased with what he saw.

Gotta get moving. I sure don't want to be running late to the station today. There's no way they'll believe

10

I overslept. Most of them probably saw me run past their houses.

Once his hair was rough-dried with a towel, he checked the time and realized that if he left now, he'd have time to drop by On Bitter Grounds on his way to the station. A large cup of steaming hot coffee with cream was just what he needed before a long shift— one of the Sweet sisters' delicious cream cheese bagels wouldn't hurt either. A little post-run carb loading would be good right now.

Of course, making a short stop and detour for coffee and bagels have nothing to do with the lovely Kari Sweet. In a town full of ordinary folks, she stood out. She had always been beautiful in Hunter's eyes, but like a fine wine she only got better with age.

They'd been flirting openly but neither had wanted to rock the boat and suggest going on a date. But maybe, just maybe, that would be a good plan.

Let's be honest, she's gorgeous, and she's super nice. What are you waiting for, man?

As Hunter tied his work shoes and clipped on his badge, his thoughts turned to just what it was about her character that he liked so much. She was kind of perfect: beautiful, smart, driven, and most importantly, fun to be around.

He knew he should ask her out; they would have fun. But what if she didn't feel the same way?

What if all the attention was just for show? Trying to make a customer happy? What if he wasn't really her type?

With all this back and forth, Hunter almost felt like going for another run to clear his head again. He'd been thinking about his future a lot lately; he was feeling the pull of settling down and making a real life for himself right here in Mills Township. Kari would be the perfect person to build that life with.

He just couldn't work out if all that flirting was simply a sales tactic she used to move more product.

I really need to find a hobby. This job is making me bitter and jaded, he thought to himself as he closed the front door.

It was a beautiful spring morning, the sky was clear though there was still quite a nip in the air, and the sound of birds singing away in the trees was refreshing to hear after a long hard winter.

I should just bite the bullet and ask her out, he thought to himself.

He remembered his high school days when his body seemed to be fighting against him.

He had fallen for Kari Sweet—and hard. He desperately wanted to ask her out, but for some reason, every time he tried to talk to her, something dorky came out of his mouth.

He remembered a particularly awful moment when he hadn't been able to force a single word out in reply to some simple question she'd asked. Instead, he ran away and hid in embarrassment. Things were different now, though.

I'm not that shy backward kid anymore.

Babe, his dark blue Silverado pickup that he named after the fabled 'Babe the Blue Ox' was waiting faithfully for him in the driveway, ready to haul him off to work—after his stop at On Bitter Grounds, of course.

He started the ignition, smiling contently and taking a moment to appreciate the growl of the engine. He dropped it in reverse and headed down the drive and onto the road.

Kari's coffee shop wasn't that far out of his way, and those bagels really were worth the effort.

Man, the place is packed this morning. Maybe I should've cut my run a little short so that I could get here earlier.

He found a parking space around the corner from the store.

It seemed the good people of Mills Township had all headed to the Sweet sisters' coffee house that morning. He climbed out of Babe, locked the door through habit and a good few years of experience in the world of law enforcement, and jogged the few steps around the corner and along the sidewalk to the shop.

Geez, there's no one on the street. Wonder if it's the weather or if I'm about to have to stand in a long line.

It was eerily quiet outside this morning, but he suspected he was about to find out why. He never knew if it was down to the outstanding coffee or the owners themselves that drew big crowds.

But as he pushed open the shop's door, his worst fears were realized—the place was booming. The line of customers was almost out the door and both Kari and Kasi were obviously flustered behind the counter—Kari working the coffee machine and Kasi doing her best to keep everyone happy as they waited at the cash register.

Maybe if I bring Jo a coffee and bagel, she won't be so upset that I'm not my usual overly punctual self? She does love a good cup of coffee, especially when it means she doesn't have to drink the stuff from the station break room for a while.

14

As he resigned himself to the fact that he wasn't going to make it to work as early as he had hoped, he caught the eye of Kari as she turned away from the machine to check on the growing line of customers.

As she turned, Hunter managed to fire a lightning-fast wink in her direction. Kari immediately blushed, and Hunter knew that his faithful killer wink had powers even he didn't quite understand.

That won't do anything to help her flustered state now, will it?

Yup, today is the day…There's no way she could turn me down.

He smiled broadly as he readied himself to ask the burning question. Today was the day, and Hunter knew it was his for the taking.

Chapter 3

Kari

Kari wiped at the perspiration forming on her brow. Though spring was well underway and truly springing, the weather outside had been cool of late. Inside On Bitter Grounds, however, things were really heating up.

The morning was proving to be a busy one, if the constant pinging of the cash register and the fact that Kari hadn't left the espresso machine alone in over half an hour were anything to go by.

The counter ran along the back wall of the shop, with a door leading to the back room. The main shop's floor was populated with cute, round tables with chairs in pairs. The girls had added a few bigger tables for four people once the shop really started to take off.

They found that lots of families and groups of school friends were using On Bitter Grounds as a weekly hangout.

Behind her, Kari could hear the contented murmuring of patient customers. Because everyone in Mills Township knew everyone else, waiting in line in stores gave people a great time to reconnect and catch up with the local gossip—all good natured, of course.

Thankful that she had her sister working with her, Kari smiled to herself as she heard Kasi talking with customers. Kasi had been alternating between manning the counter and bussing tables.

With long straight brown hair and beautiful hazel eyes, Kasi was really gorgeous, and Kari was proud to be her sister. Fixated on tamping down ground coffee for the next customer, Kari didn't realize Kasi had disappeared into the prep room to fix an order. Kari was also surprised when she heard a familiar deep voice pulling her from her coffee reverie.

"Any chance of a little service around here?" came the voice of none other than Kari's favorite customer, Officer Hunter Houston.

Glad that the killer wink accompanying his demand showed he wasn't one of those customers, Kari smiled back as she wiped her coffee-ground-covered hands on her On Bitter Grounds branded apron, which covered her jeans and most of her long-sleeved baby blue t-shirt. A little dismayed, however, that she had tied her curly hair back out of the way that morning, Kari turned back to the coffee machine.

Determined to get the ever-growing line of customers moving, she picked up the pace and made the coffee machine work harder than it ever had before.

Seeing that Kasi had not returned from the prep room, Kari chanced a peek to see what she was up to.

"Hey, Kasi, need a little help out front!" she called to her sister.

"Sure, hold up, I'm coming!" Kasi replied as she grabbed the to-go bags she had been preparing.

She ambled out into the shop and immediately noticed the fine form of her sister's current flirting partner.

"Oh, I see," she said with a twinkle in her eye, "you need my help out here."

Kari continued valiantly pouring shots of delicious black coffee, while simultaneously steaming milk and adding foam to the growing list of orders. The scent of freshly brewed coffee filled the air, warming her soul from the inside out. As she worked, she managed to peek back to keep tabs on where Hunter was in the queue.

She watched a second too long as he busied himself with a look-see at all the delicious pastries displayed on the counter. Before she even noticed what was happening, Kari poured freshly steamed milk over the edge of a cup and over her hand.

"Ow!" she cried, running for the hand basin in the prep room.

As soon as she re-emerged from fixing her hand, Kari's arrival at the shop counter coincided with Hunter's turn at the front of the line. Kari waited a minute as he finished shuffling some sugar sachets in their container.

Was he… nervous?

Watching everything that was going on, Kasi whispered slyly to her sister with the back of her hand covering her mouth, "Doesn't he have any criminal to catch?!"

"Not yet at least," Hunter said, smiling, suddenly very present and too close for comfort. "How are you today Kari?" he continued innocently, ignoring the fact that he had caught them talking about him.

As Kari shoved her sister back into the prep room, she composed herself into the professional barista that she was, even if she might have looked just a little ruffled. She smoothed her apron and tucked an errant strand of lose hair back behind her ear.

"Oh, hi, Hunter," Kari replied, caught off guard and blushing. "What uh…Would you like your usual? Or can I tempt you into a delicious mocha latte and a breakfast special bagel with cream cheese—all home-made right here of course. Isn't that right, Kasi?"

"That's right, Kari," Kasi replied from the back, unable to hide the amusement in her voice.

Kari was glad Kasi wasn't too close. If she had caught her sister's eye at this point, she knew it would only end in a fit of the giggles, and that wouldn't be the impression she wanted to make at all.

"Oh, I think I'll stick with the old faithful, just a coffee with cream. On second thought, I think I'll take that bagel, too, which sounded good. Oh, to go, please," he said, smiling.

"Well, you don't need to worry about too many carbs at least!" Kari replied in a clumsy attempt to amuse Hunter.

"Huh?" Hunter replied, looking genuinely perplexed by her statement.

"I mean, it's just that I saw you out running this morning. It looked like you were really going for it," she answered, flushed and confused by the terrible confusion she felt inside.

She wanted to compliment Hunter but had foolishly let her mouth run ahead of her thoughts. He was in great shape, but she also knew he was a great runner with a regular exercise schedule.

"Oh, right, I see. You're not…you're not stalking me, are you, Kari?" he replied with twinkling eyes.

Kasi chose that exact moment to reappear with Hunter's to-go bag ready in her hand, the shop's logo proudly displayed on the front.

"Hey, thanks, Kasi. How are you doing today?" he said, taking the bag from Kari's younger sister.

"Oh, just great—at least I'll be when I get the chance to sneak out for a little breakfast myself!" she replied, rubbing her tummy as she spoke before turning to wipe the counter so she could pretend like she had important tasks that needed her immediate attention right there next to her sister and Hunter.

"That's too bad. And what about you, Kari? Did you manage to get your breakfast this morning?"

"Oh, no. I'm not a fan of breakfast. Just a latte does it for me usually!" Kari replied.

"What?! No breakfast? Don't you know it's the most important meal of the day? Breakfast like a king— isn't that what they say?" he said, pretending to be shocked to his core. "You need to start eating, Kari Sweet, or you'll fade away."

Kari laughed as she keyed in his order on the cash register, enjoying his gentle teasing.

"As a matter of fact, to make sure you start eating breakfast for real, what would you say to joining me tomorrow morning at Sally's Diner before work?"

Kari stood frozen, her hand hovering above the register's keypad. Fortunately, Kasi was ready to leap into action to spare Hunter's blushes and prevent her sister from making a big mistake, thanks to her social glitch.

"She'd love to, Hunter," she said, turning to elbow her sister in the ribs. "Wouldn't you, Kari?"

Kari managed to nod dumbly, sure that her mouth was still hanging open.

"It's a date, then!" he said as he placed the exact change for his coffee and bagel into Kari's open hand.

To-go bag in hand, Hunter turned to leave the shop with a new spring in his step.

Just as he reached out to grab the door handle, Kari managed to find her voice once again.

"Wh-what time?" she stuttered.

"Meet you at six," Hunter replied confidently, with that million-dollar smile of his.

And with a jingle of the bell above the door, he was gone. Kari and Kasi turned to each other with matching expressions of surprise before they burst out laughing.

Did that whole thing just happen for real? Did Hunter Houston really ask her out?

Chapter 4

Kari

Kari immediately turned to her sister. "What just happened?!" she asked in shock.

"You, dear sister," Kasi began as she wiped away the coffee grounds covering Kari's apron, "just accepted a date with Mills Township's most handsome police officer. That's what!"

Kari and Kasi broke into fits of giggles once again, neither of them quite able to believe everything that had already gone down that morning. With a cough from one of the On Bitter Grounds customers, they were reminded that they were in their place of work.

So, they tried to pull themselves together—knowing full well that if either one of them had caught the other's eye, giggles would erupt once again.

Thanks to Hunter's public date proposal, everyone in the coffee house was looking their way, eager to see what might happen next.

"Alright people, nothing to see here…go back to your coffee," Kari said, with the intention of redirecting the very glaring limelight of which she was no fan.

If the smirks on the faces of her customers were anything to go by, Kari was in for a day of it.

One of the best and worst things about life in Mills Township was the speed with which any kind of news—good or bad—could be shared among its inhabitants. Kari knew full well that she and Hunter would be the hot topic of conversation all over town.

***

Kari and Kasi spent the rest of their day alternating between roasting coffee beans and tending to their valued customers. Thankful that the intensity of that morning's rush didn't keep up for the remainder of the day, the girls set about their work in peaceful harmony so much so that they were both genuinely surprised to discover that it was already just about five o'clock.

Kari had spent much of the day pondering her memories of Hunter from way back, when they had attended high school together. He'd been so shy and awkward back then. It had felt like every time she had tried to engage him in conversation in a class they had shared together, he had clammed up and turned bright red.

He had really changed since then—a lot. Kari had to admit, she was quite glad about that and about some of the physical changes he'd gone through, too. The teenage Hunter of yesterday was no match for the fine figure he cut these days.

Ready to roll out the door and relax for the evening, Kari made a quick, last check of their website to see if new orders had arrived before she shut down the computer and gladly switched off the coffee machine.

At the same time, Kasi began turning off the various lights they had around the store and gave the counter one final wipe, so it was ready to go the next morning. In silence, the girls closed the door, locking it carefully behind them and headed out into the chilly spring evening.

Upon reaching Kari's orange four-door Jeep Wrangler with the black hard-top, the girls began to debate where they should head for dinner. Keen to stay as far away from the kitchen as much as they could, eating out was the best decision after the hectic and eventful day.

"How about we just head down the street and eat at Taste of Venice?" Kari suggested.

"Ooh, good call—I love their lasagna!"

"It's great, right?" Kari was almost drooling in anticipation of the salad and lasagna she was picturing in her mind.

"Woah, it's busy tonight, huh!" Kasi exclaimed as they circled the block again, looking for a vacant parking slot.

It seemed like the entire population of Mills Township was out and about that evening.

"Sure is! I guess we'll just park right here and take a stroll to the restaurant. I'm starving!"

As soon as the evening set in, the temperature seemed to drop, and the girls started to shiver as they hurried toward Taste of Venice. Pushing the door open, the warmth of the restaurant immediately hit them, making them feel instantly at home and keen to eat. The restaurant always smelled so good it was hard to keep from drooling.

"Hey there, Kari. Hey, Kasi! Come on in, two for diner?" the restaurant's owner, Cindy King asked as they crossed the threshold. "I have a great table for you back here," she continued as she directed the Sweet sisters toward a beautifully laid out booth near the back of the room, the perfect spot for a little post-work debrief.

"Hey, thanks, Cindy. We're so hungry! Can we order right away? We already know what we want," Kari said as she shrugged out of her jacket and took her seat.

Kasi nodded in agreement as she sat down.

"Sure you can, ladies. What can I get for you?"

"Well, I'm going to go for the house salad with ranch dressing, followed by your great lasagna and meat sauce, please," Kari said.

"Sure. And Kasi, what can I get you?"

"Hah! I'm going to have the same, please. You just can't beat your lasagna, Cindy!" Kasi replied.

"And your drinks, girls?" Cindy asked.

"Oh, sure, how about two hot teas with sugar?" Kari asked as she nodded toward her sister for her agreement.

"Great, I'll tell the kitchen and get that right out to you, girls," Cindy said as she finished scribbling their order on her notepad.

As soon as their hot tea arrived, Kari took a small sip, blowing at the surface in order to cool it first. It seemed as though Kasi had other ideas, however, as she immediately began to dig at her sister.

"Don't eat too much tonight. You might not want any breakfast tomorrow morning," she all but whispered as she rearranged the cutlery laid out on their table.

"What?!"

"You know, Hunter would want to see you chow down on a nice stack of pancakes. You heard what he said, he's worried that you might fade away!" she teased.

"Kasi, hush! I don't want everyone to know about this!"

"I think it might be too late, sis," Kasi said as she gestured to the rest of the restaurant.

It seemed like word had indeed spread like wildfire that day. More than one of the other tables in the restaurant seemed to be smiling in Kari's direction.

"Great, that's all I need," Kari said.

She couldn't help thinking about the following morning and was powerless against the blush she could feel rising across her cheeks. What was it about the simplest mention of Hunter that made her react this way?

"I just can't get over how much he has changed since high school," Kari mused out loud.

"I know, right? He's gorgeous now that he's all grown up! I remember him being so dorky back in school."

"I know! He was so shy! Every time I tried to speak to him in class, he'd turn bright red and just shut

28

down." Kari laughed at the memory of a particularly painful science class.

"What I want to know is just how he turned out so well. What happened?!" Kasi teased.

"Who knows? But I'm glad he's done with his ugly duckling phase. And I'm so glad we reconnected."

"Agreed. I can't believe you two are actually going out on a date tomorrow morning!"

At the reminder, Kari swallowed hard. There was so much to consider.

What was she going to wear? What would she eat?

Normally a fan of a simple cup of coffee in the morning rather than anything more complex, she had no idea what she might choose and for some reason, this was only adding to the nerves she already felt. How was she going to get any sleep tonight?

Somehow, she managed to squash down the butterflies in her stomach as she chatted with her sister. They both enjoyed their well-earned evening meal.

By the time the girls had their fill and had the leftovers boxed up, it was nearing 6:30 p.m. After paying up and returning to Kari's car, all that was left was to return home and try to pick out something appropriate to wear for Kari's date the next morning—just a few hours away.

Chapter 5

Kari

With full bellies, sated and content, Kari and Kasi meandered leisurely back down the street to the Jeep. Taking their time, they both used the spot of unexpected leisure time to enjoy their surroundings and do a little window shopping.

With the upswing in their business of late, both online and in real-life, neither woman had had much time to check out any new items in the stores.

Business had been so hectic that the girls had been working long hours trying to deal with the customers and sales coming their way from the On Bitter Grounds website. Not that they minded; things were going so well for them. It was, however, definitely time for a new season wardrobe refresh.

Both Sweet sisters really enjoyed shopping for new clothes. They both loved fashion and trying out new looks.

As much as Kari admired her sister, she knew she looked pretty good, too. Kari worked hard at staying in great shape and she certainly enjoyed dressing her tall, lean figure as well as she could.

She liked clothes she could live in day-to-day, clothes that flattered her subtle curves and were practical too.

Stylish outfits that could withstand being sprayed with stray coffee grounds were ideal. She needed items that were wash and wear but looked chic.

It had just been such a long time since either of them had the time to check out new fashions. Of course, the great benefit of having a sister was that you got double the wardrobe for half the money. While they mostly happily agreed to borrow clothes, there were occasional arguments over the true owner of a particular item of clothing.

Kari thought back to one particularly heated discussion as to the original owner of that cute blouse with pink embroidered flowers…

She wondered what had happened to that one.

As they came across their favorite boutique in town, Style Factory, both Kari and Kasi stopped to admire the display of cute spring dresses and capris in the window. They were exactly the kind of outfits both sisters liked to wear— stylish yet casual, smart but comfortable.

Even if the winter weather has dragged on longer than usual, the first buds of spring surely were just around the corner, and cute dresses and capris were the perfect items of clothing to cheer up a slow start to the new season.

Almost under her breath, Kari spoke with a longing for a bright new wardrobe, "Too bad they're already closed. We could've asked Lila to put some of those gorgeous dresses and pants on hold for us."

"It looks like the light is still on in the back. Maybe she's still in there," Kasi replied.

"We could knock. She might just hear us from here" Kari suggested, almost hopefully.

In Kari's mind, there was nothing better than something just a little out of the ordinary. She had always been secretly proud of her keen observation skills and had always loved a juicy mystery—even if they often turned out to be nothing too zany after all.

She and Kasi had spent long hours playing in the back yard when they were kids, pretending to be investigators. They had both loved watching Scooby Doo, even though their parents thought it might have been too scary for young children.

Kari remembered when their cat had gone missing. She spent ages looking for clues and dusting for fingerprints with the investigator kit she received as a birthday present.

Could this be lining up to be a mystery for real? she wondered, half joking to herself.

She was almost certain there would be a simple explanation. Lila probably just forgot to turn off the light when she left the store.

Kasi knocked gently on the window and waited a second for Lila to respond before she knocked again, this time with a little more force.

"Wait, Kari. What was that? I swear I saw Lila move back there," Kasi said, then paused for a second. "Maybe it was just a shadow?" she whispered as she placed her hand instinctively on her sister's arm.

"Let's knock again," Kari replied cautiously.

She moved toward the door to knock harder, and after another second of waiting, there was still no response nor movement in the store. She was getting more convinced that they had stumbled across a real-life mystery.

"Are you sure you saw something, Kasi? I can't see anyone back there," she said as she peered through the door's glass.

"I swear, Kari, I saw someone moving…I don't know. Looked a little too big to be Lila."

Kari felt a shiver along the back of her neck, an uneasy feeling spreading throughout her body. With more than a little trepidation and a bravery she never guessed she had, she pushed at the door to check if it was unlocked.

With a turn of the handle, the door opened. Curious, the girls ventured into the interior of the shop.

"Lila? Lila! Is that you back there?" Kari called out cautiously, a barely-there crack in her voice.

This was it; it was really happening—an actual mystery.

"Maybe she can't hear us from out here," Kasi whispered, hesitation in her voice. "Let's go further in. Maybe she's deep in a pile of boxes or something?"

Deciding to jettison the growing unease gnawing at her, Kari walked further into the store and called out with a confidence that called on the best of her acting skills.

"Hey, Lila! Are you back there? It's just us, Kari and Kasi!" she called brightly. "Did you know that you left your door unlocked?"

She waited a second for a response then called out again, "Lila?"

With no answer forthcoming, Kari couldn't help swallowing the lump of fear making its presence felt in her throat. She instinctively felt that something wasn't right.

For all her childhood dreams of solving a real crime, when it came down to it, Kari wasn't sure she wanted to play along anymore. She held out her hand to grab Kasi's outstretched one, and together, they stepped toward the stock room and the source of their concern.

Inching closer, the girls peeked around the open door of Lila's stock room. At that moment, they knew that life in Mills Township—their idyll of small-town safety—would never be the same again.

On the floor before them lay the lifeless body of Lila Baldwin.

With lightning-fast reaction, Kasi reached into her purse and pulled out her cellphone in one swift move. She punched in 911.

Kari stared dumbfounded at the body of one of the town's most respected businesswomen.

The world around her seemed to freeze, and everything became muffled except for the sound of her own deep and slow breath. Her ears could only hear a strange whooshing noise, and every muscle in her body was rigid—ready to go, fight or flight.

Within moments, Kari started to come around, and she became aware of her sister speaking into her phone. Her whole body was shaking from the shock.

Shaking her head to clear it, Kari snapped to full awareness of the very real and dangerous situation in which they had found themselves.

"Kasi, come on, we need to get out of here. If you did see someone, they might still be here," she whispered, as her eyes darted around the room, assessing the risk and the potential of an unseen threat.

She grabbed her sister, and together they backed out of Lila's store, arms linked for comfort and safety.

Just as they were about to clear the threshold of the shop and run for the safety of the Jeep, a police car pulled up alongside the store. Breathing a huge sigh of relief, Kari couldn't help smiling nervously when she saw just who it was that climbed out of the cruiser.

"Looks like your date might be starting a little early, sis." Kasi said in a voice tinged with fear and apprehension.

Kari didn't think she'd ever been more grateful to see anyone in her life. Standing before her was all six two of Hunter Houston—a sight for sore eyes indeed.

Chapter 6

Hunter

Hunter sat there, frozen, with the mic of his car radio in hand. He couldn't process what he was hearing. The call had just come over the radio saying that Lila Baldwin was dead in her shop.

And if that wasn't enough, the Sweet sisters were the ones who found her.

This just doesn't make any sense, he thought. Things like this don't happen in Mills Township.

It felt like an eternity, but in reality, only seconds passed before Hunter's training kicked in. He waited for a break in the radio calls of the other units who announced they were responding before keying the mic and relaying that he was on his way as well.

Hunter didn't think they'd have any trouble securing the scene when he got there. It sounded like every unit that was out was going to show up, and there was little wonder in that.

His mind kept repeating it, Things like this don't happen in this sleepy little town.

He threw his patrol vehicle in gear and figured out the fastest route to Lila's boutique. He switched on his lights and sirens as he sped across town, the foreign sound and reflection serving as just one more reminder of how odd this situation was.

As he pulled up to the building, the glow from the other patrol cars' headlights and roof racks illuminated Kari and Kasi, who were just coming out the front doors. Kasi was holding a plastic bag with what looked like food containers in it. Both seemed a little shaken, which came as no surprise.

Discovering a dead body could have a profoundly traumatic effect on people. Despite his training to not allow personal feelings to cloud his judgment, he couldn't ignore the fact that his first thought upon seeing the girls was to run over and hug Kari.

He wanted to make sure she was okay. But he knew that he had a job to do and that would have to wait.

Hunter jumped out of the car almost before he finished putting it in park. He rushed over to the sisters, calling out, "Kari! Kasi! Are you girls okay? What happened?"

The girls both looked at him, clearly not knowing where to start.

As they took deep breaths, Hunter saw they were both about to start speaking at the same time. He held up both hands to stop them.

"Okay, okay. First things first, are you hurt?"

Both girls released their breath and shook their heads.

"Okay, good." He let out a sigh of relief.

Before he could ask them anything else, another officer approached.

Teddy Layne had been with the department longer than Hunter had, and he knew from the dispatcher he had been the first officer on the scene.

"Officer Houston, why don't we have the girls wait in the patrol cars while we secure the scene?" Teddy said.

Hunter nodded in agreement and led Kari to his car. He saw that Teddy was doing the same with Kasi. He knew the girls had to be split up so they could be questioned separately as witnesses, but he didn't know how the sisters would interpret it.

"It's gonna be alright," he told Kari as he got her settled. "The car is nice and warm, so just wait here while we make sure it's safe."

Kari just nodded in agreement.

Hunter saw that two other officers, Smith and Miller, had joined the group and were getting orders form Teddy. As he approached them, he caught the end of what they were saying.

"...while you and Officer Miller are checking the left, Officer Houston and I will head around to the right side of the building," Teddy was saying. "Remember, we don't know what's going on in there. All we know is that there's a report of a body. We don't know if this was a natural death, an accidental one, or homicide. We don't know if she's alone or if there was someone else with her, and we don't know if there's still someone hiding in there. So, keep your eyes open and touch as little as you can. We don't want to contaminate the scene any more than we have to."

The two officers nodded. Hunter could see in their faces they were nervous, and he knew he must be wearing a similar expression.

Teddy turned to Hunter. "Did you get all that, Houston?" At Hunter's nod, he said, "Alright. Let's go."

Teddy pulled out his sidearm, and the three other officers unholstered theirs as well. They headed toward the door in a crouch-walk, and two of them flanked either side of the door. Teddy checked one final time that the other officers were ready, then signaled a countdown with his hand and pulled the door open.

The officers quickly went through the shop and determined that no intruders were present.

Once the scene had been cleared, they focused on Lila's body.

She was lying on her left side and appeared to have been stabbed in the stomach. Teddy knelt beside her and checked for a pulse. After a moment, he shook his head.

Teddy sighed audibly as he pulled his radio from his belt, keyed the mic, and requested dispatch to send a coroner.

After hearing the confirmation from Sally at dispatch, Teddy turned to the other officers. "Officer Smith, I want this place taped off. Officer Miller, I want pictures of everything in here. Officer Houston and I will go interview the witnesses."

Before Hunter could get back to the cars, Teddy stopped him.

"We have to find out what these girls were doing here, why they were here, and if they had something to do with this," he said.

Hunter was shaking his head before he even started to answer. "Teddy, this is Kari and Kasi. They run the coffee shop, On Bitter Grounds. They're good people. I can't imagine they'd be involved."

He remembered Kari's adorable smile as she handed him his bagel and cream cheese. There was no way she could hurt anyone.

Teddy held his hands. "Hunter, I get it. They serve me my coffee every day too, just the same as you, and far more breakfasts than my wife would approve of or needs to know anything about. I don't think those two are killers any more than you do, but we have a job to do. Should I have someone else question Kari?"

"No, I'll interview Kari. It's not a problem. I just don't think it was them."

"Okay, go talk to her, and see what she has to say. Keep an open mind. I'll interview her sister." Teddy turned and started to walk away before he turned back and added, "Remember to go easy with her. Outside of a funeral, this is probably the first dead body she has ever seen."

Hunter nodded and walked to his own car. He hesitated for just a second before opening the door. As he got into the front of his patrol car, he tried not to think about how vulnerable Kari looked and how wrong it was to have her in the back of the patrol car.

No, I can't think about that right now. I can't think about how much I just want to hold her and how much I've been looking forward to having breakfast with her tomorrow morning.

43

Kari was wide-eyed when he got in the car, like she was waiting for him to say something, to let her know that this was all just a big misunderstanding.

But Hunter had a feeling that she knew, before he got back to the car, that this wasn't the case. Lila was really dead.

"Kari, I have to ask you some questions."

She laughed nervously. Hunter figured she couldn't help herself. The whole situation was just too surreal.

She collected herself quickly and said, "I'm sorry. Of course, you do."

"It's okay. It's actually not an uncommon reaction. Well, that's what we were taught. I don't have a lot of experience in this."

Hunter realized that he was speaking as if the two of them were friends having a conversation and he's not an officer of the law taking an official statement.

His tone and demeanor changed to business-like. "What were you and Kasi doing here, Kari?"

Kari told Hunter about how they went out to dinner and were doing a little window shopping afterward. They had wanted to put some items on hold at the Style Factory, so they knocked on the window to get Lila's attention, then realized the door was unlocked.

Since the light was on, they'd gone in and found her in the back room.

That was when they called 911, and before they could get back out, Hunter and the other cops had already shown up.

Nothing about her story gave Hunter any inclination she was lying. "How do you and Kasi know Lila?"

"We're pretty good friends with her and have been for a long time. We've been in the boutique plenty of times, and she comes to the shop to get coffee. She even gave us some tips when we first opened On Bitter Grounds. And, you know, it's a small town, so everybody knows everybody."

"So, you thought she would open the shop for you two after hours?"

"Well…" Kari hesitated for a moment. "We didn't really think that she'd open the shop. We just thought that maybe she'd let us reserve some things so that we could take a look at them another time. We don't often get out during business hours. When we saw the light on, we thought maybe she'd do us the favor, you know, shop keep to shop keep."

Hunter nodded. It made sense. He knew the girls started working early in the morning and were often there all day.

He thanked her for explaining it to him and asked her a few questions about her and Kasi's relationship with Lila and if they knew of anyone who wanted to hurt her.

"I don't even know anyone who didn't like her," Kari told him truthfully.

Hunter saw Teddy climb out of his cruiser, and he told Kari he'd be back in a minute. He got out of his car and walked over to where Teddy was waiting for him.

"Kasi said that the two of them went out to A Taste of Venice for lasagna and salad, and they did a little window shopping after they ate. She said they saw a few things they wanted to put on hold, and seeing the light on in the back room, they knocked on the door and realized it was unlocked. She thought she saw a shadow, and thinking it was Lila, they went in. Getting no response to their calls, they went in the back, and that was when they found her. She called 911, and then they met us outside. What did Kari say?"

"The same. Stories match up."

"Yeah, I kind of figured they would. We'll follow up with the 911 operator they spoke to and the waitress from A Taste of Venice to corroborate their story, but you can still smell the leftovers in her bag. Okay, I'll go get Kasi. Would you bring Kari out here?"

Hunter nodded and returned to the vehicle to let her out.

When the four of them were together, Teddy addressed the girls. "Thank you both for your statements and cooperation. If you think of anything else at all, please call us immediately."

"Okay," Kari said.

"Will do," Kasi replied, still holding the bag of leftovers in her hand.

"I can give you a ride to your car," Hunter said.

The girls both nodded and followed him.

The ride to the jeep was silent but thankfully quick. Both the Sweet girls thanked Hunter for taking them.

He wanted to tell Kari that he'd see her in the morning, but he didn't know if it was the right time. He just hoped she would be at Sally's when he got there.

After they climbed in the jeep and drove away, Hunter went back to the Style Factory. He took a deep breath and let it out slowly before getting out of the car. This was going to be a long night.

Chapter 7

Kari

In silence, Kari and Kasi drove back to their house on Mulberry Lane. They couldn't think of anything other than Lila Baldwin lying there on the floor.

Lila had been a good friend to the sisters. She had always been there for them for a quick coffee and chat or when they needed expert business advice during the early days of On Bitter Grounds.

Who could have done such a thing to a lovely woman like her? More importantly, why would anyone do such a thing?

Seeing a dead body was one thing, but seeing the body of a friend, someone both girls admired and looked up to, was something else altogether. Lila had been one of their first regulars at On Bitter Grounds, and the Sweet sisters had been so glad to have her company and support.

Kari couldn't put a value on Lila's words of wisdom. Not only had she helped them answer tough business questions, but she also helped them see how a small town like Mills Township operated on the business side. What Kari remembered most, though, was that Lila gave advice kind-heartedly and with a smile.

As Kari turned into Mulberry Street and made her way toward their home, she was grateful for the silence filling the Jeep. She guessed that Kasi was busy processing what had happened and what they had seen, just as she was. It was hard to imagine how such a lovely evening and dinner had turned so ugly in a span of a few minutes.

As the girls climbed out of the Jeep in the driveway, Kasi busied herself by grabbed her purse from the foot-well of the car and brushed down the seat for non-existent crumbs.

It seemed to Kari that Kasi was delaying going inside their home for as long as possible, as if doing so would make Lila's death more real and permanent somehow.

Once Kasi had closed the car door, Kari stretched her arm out to take her younger sister's hand in a show of solidarity.

"I'm okay, Kari," Kasi said, squeezing her hand. "I just can't get my head around why anyone would do such a thing to such a lovely woman."

"I know. I feel the exact same way. I just don't understand."

Lila had been such a vibrant and friendly woman. She always welcomed each customer into her shop with a kind face and a warm heart.

"Remember that time when you needed a new scarf when it was, like, twenty below outside?" Kari asked her sister.

Kasi smiled. "Yep. She helped me find the most beautiful, warmest scarf in the store. And the whole time I was trying them on, she brought me cup after cup of hot coffee."

Kari nodded. "She almost made everyone who came in feel like a million dollars. She really was a very special lady."

"Do you know if she had any family?" Kari asked as she unlocked the front door.

"I don't think so," Kasi replied sadly.

"Nobody close to her that she might have spoken about?" Kari continued as the pair dumped their bags in the hallway, ready for another early start the next morning.

Kasi went into the kitchen to stash the leftovers of their meal in the fridge.

"Wait," she called from the kitchen, "I'm sure I remember her talking about an elderly aunt who lives in the assisted living facility in town. But apart from her, I don't think there was anyone. Poor thing."

"It's so sad that she never married, nor had any children. She would've been so great as a mom, right?" Kari replied as the sisters met again in the living room, switching the lights on as they went.

"I guess so. The only bright side of it is that if she had decided on a family, and if she had gotten married, then there would only be more people mourning her loss and grieving for her right now. So sad."

"You make a good point," Kari said, pausing for a moment. "Well, I'm going upstairs to take a shower, clean up a little, and relax, you know?"

"Yeah, I'll go after you—a nice hot shower might be just what the doctor ordered."

***

After taking her shower and putting on her most comfortable robe, Kari had to admit she felt worlds better. She went downstairs to find her sister and see if she was in the mood to hash out more details about Lila's case.

Kasi was on the phone and, by the sound of things, she was speaking with their father, Aaron Sweet. Kari listened in on Kasi's half of the conversation but couldn't quite get the gist.

While she waited for her sister to finish the call, she noticed that Kasi had also dressed in a big fluffy robe.

She also had on the fuzzy slippers that Kari had gotten her the previous Christmas.

"Was that Dad?" Kari asked as Kasi hung up the phone.

"Yeah, and Mom. I told them what happened before they could hear it from anyone else. You know how fast bad news travels around here. Dad said he'd come over if we need him to and spend the night if we were scared."

"Oh, that's so nice of him. What did you say?"

"I said that we'd be okay, we have each other." Kasi gave her a smile. "We're adults now. We can't have Daddy running over to take care of us each time something bad happens."

"Yeah, but it would have been nice though." Kari wrapped her arms around her sister. "I'm really glad you're here, sis. Everything is easier when we're together."

Kasi squeezed her back. "Right back at ya, Kari. What are your thoughts on a movie? I think I just want to…take my mind off things right now."

Though she'd been hoping to discuss some possible suspects in Lila's murder, Kari admitted that this was probably not a good time to do so. Relaxing and spending time together doing something completely unrelated to the case was definitely a better idea.

Kari left her sister flicking through potential movies and went into the kitchen to reheat their Taste of Venice leftovers. Maybe something tasty and delicious would also be a welcome distraction.

Kari watched the box of leftover lasagne as it turned slowly in the microwave, distracted for a second by the monotony of it. Once the microwave dinged, she plated up their meals, grabbed a pair of forks, and rejoined her sister in the living room.

"Here, Kasi, try and eat something," Kari said, handing her sister a plate. "Nothing like some good ol' comfort food to make you feel better."

"Okay," Kasi said sadly. "I'll take a little bit, I guess."

Kasi and Kari both pushed at the food on their plates. Not even the best that Taste of Venice had to offer could distract them from their thoughts.

"How about One Fine Day?" Kari asked, scrolling through the movie list. "It's got George Clooney in it."

"Okay, perhaps a little bit of Mr. Clooney might distract us for a while anyway," Kasi replied.

As the movie started, the girls both put their feet up on the couch so their legs were touching. It's something they had done since they were little kids and when one of them needed comforting or cheering up. Sometimes just being close was all they needed to get through a tough time.

Since neither of them seemed too inclined to go to their own rooms to sleep, they stayed up until almost midnight, until they were too tired to keep their eyes open.

Kari remembered she had a breakfast date in the morning; otherwise, she might have opted to sleep on the couch with her sister.

"I think I'm going to head up," she told Kasi as the credits rolled. "I've got to be up at 5 a.m."

"I'll go with you." Kasi turned off the television and followed her sister up the stairs. "Kar? I love you, you know that, right?"

"I love you, too, Kasi." She hugged her sister tightly. "It'll all be okay. You'll see."

But the truth was, she wasn't all that sure. A murder occurred in their little pocket of the world, and nothing would ever be the same.

Chapter 8

Kari

Kari didn't really need her alarm clock that morning, despite the early hour. After a late night followed by fitful sleep, she was already awake and waiting peacefully for confirmation that the day was about to begin when her alarm clock went off.

Partly due to lack of sleep, and partly due to the anticipation of her breakfast date with Hunter, she had no trouble getting herself into the bathroom to begin getting ready for the day ahead. She showered and brushed her teeth before she headed back to her bedroom to get dressed.

After a few minutes hunting through her wardrobe, she eventually opted for a pair of dark denim jeans and a red long-sleeved top that she had bought to support the local cheerleading squad at Mills Township High School.

Once she was dressed, she began the daily battle with her hair. She loved her curls but didn't enjoy the upkeep and care it took to make sure they looked their best every day. She ran some serum through the lengths then dried her hair on the slow setting gently and carefully allowed each section to dry before moving to the next.

She then brushed through her long brown hair with her favorite big brush, made just for curly hair. After that, she smoothed her hair through one final time.

Would she wear it down or tie it up? She did have another long day ahead in On Bitter Grounds; that's why she didn't think she could stand her hair getting in the way, especially if they were going to be as busy as they had been of late.

It wasn't until 5:30 a.m. that she heard her sister stir. By then, Kari was almost ready to leave. She put the finishing touches to her outfit by pulling her hair up into a relaxed chignon and adding a little makeup to hide the worst of the dark circles that had developed beneath her eyes.

After the evening before and the night that had followed, she had no doubt that she wouldn't make the most glamorous of impressions that morning—especially not at so early an hour. The least she could hope for was that Hunter wouldn't run away screaming at the very sight of her.

As she skipped down the stairs to grab her purse and keys, the sounds of Kasi taking a shower and getting ready filled their home. Kari remembered that Kasi would need to drive herself to On Bitter Grounds that morning, so before she headed out of the front door, she called to her sister to remind her.

"Hey, Kasi?"

No answer.

"Kasi?" she tried again.

She waited until she could no longer hear the shower running, then called up one last time—if it didn't work this time, she would leave a note.

"Kasi?"

"Morning, Kari! What's up?" Kasi finally replied.

"Don't forget you need to drive yourself to the coffee shop this morning!"

"Don't remind me! I am not looking forward to that," Kasi shouted from upstairs.

Kari laughed when she heard her sister grumbling from the direction of the bathroom. Taking this as verification that Kasi had indeed heard her, Kari recalled how reluctant her sister had always been when it came to driving herself—or anyone else for that matter—anywhere in her car.

Even when Kasi had turned sixteen—when all her friends had been desperate for the freedom that finally being able to drive gave them, Kasi had been quite happy relying on Kari and their parents to drive her anywhere she needed to go. In fact, their parents almost had to force her to go along and take the driving test when the time came.

"Hey, driving isn't so bad—especially not when you get a great car like the Jeep!" Kari called back.

"Well, I guess at least I can prove once and for all that my car gets better mileage!"

"I wouldn't be so sure about that, Kasi. It's easy to get good mileage when you do all your miles in someone else's car!" Kari replied, laughing.

This was one aspect where the Sweet sisters were totally different. Kari loved her Jeep and loved driving it. She didn't even mind the challenges brought by ice and snow during the winter—one of the reasons she had opted for the Jeep in the first place.

There wasn't a weather situation that her Jeep couldn't handle. Kasi had chosen the more practical Hyundai Tucson instead, arguing that the car she wanted had everything she needed with its all-wheel-drive feature—and it apparently got great mileage.

After skipping out of the house with a lightness in her step, Kari waited a few moments on the driveway as the Jeep warmed up then headed into town for breakfast with Hunter at Sally's Diner.

The diner wasn't too far from home. Yet another benefit that came from living in a small town—everything was within easy reach.

It was very easy to find a spot close to the little restaurant because it was still so early in the morning. Later on, things would be different, and it would be much more difficult to find a spot anywhere in town. That was one of the best things about Mills Township; though it was a small town, the people were more than generous when it came to supporting each other.

Support for local businesses was so strong, and because of the strength of the community, Kari and Kasi's coffee shop had benefitted, too. The girls were so glad for the strong community spirit of their friends and neighbors. It really made a difference in getting their business off the ground.

Of course, Kari often wondered if the collective sweet tooth of the good people of Mills Township might have had anything to do with it. The girls had more than one ardent fan of their delicious baked goods and sweet treats, and Kari was glad about that, too.

Kari was also committed to returning the favor and always tried to shop locally when possible. That was why she and her sister had loved the Style Factory, even if she hadn't had much of a chance to do any shopping of late.

Lila Baldwin had really developed a great eye for the latest trends over the years, no matter what the season. Kari was really going to miss her.

As Kari's thoughts returned to the shocking scene they had stumbled upon the previous evening, she got out of her car, locking it behind her, and headed into the diner, shaking off the early morning chill as she entered.

As soon as she walked through the door, she greeted the line cook, Daryl Simpson, who she had spotted peeking through the 'order up' window.

"Hey, Daryl! How are you today?" she asked.

"I'm great, thanks, Kari. It's a bit of an early start for you this morning, no?" he replied before heading back into the kitchen whistling a happy little tune.

Daryl had worked at Sally's Diner for twenty-five years, and Kari just couldn't imagine the diner without him. She was also pretty sure the man had never taken a day off as she couldn't even remember a visit to the diner when he hadn't been there. Taking the pick of the seats, Kari chose a table by the window so she could watch out for Hunter arriving.

As she waited, Nikki, the waitress, ambled over, bringing her a tall glass of fresh orange juice.

"Oh, hey, Nikki! Thanks. That juice looks so great!"

"Yup, freshly squeezed by Daryl this morning, as it happens. You waiting for someone else?" Nikki asked, though Kari expected she knew full well exactly whom it was she was there to meet.

When Nikki went back to the kitchen, Kari returned to her thoughts. This time, all she could think about were the butterflies starting to flap about in her belly.

Before too long had passed and Kari had a chance to work herself up any further, she spotted Hunter's blue Silverado truck pulling into a spot beside her Jeep. Now the butterflies started to fly about with renewed haste.

Noticing the dryness in her mouth as her nervousness really made itself felt, Kari gave herself a good pep talk. She needed to calm down. This wasn't some teenage date, and she simply couldn't go around behaving like her younger self had back in the day.

Now, she was a grown businesswoman who knew exactly how to behave and how to speak to all sorts of people. After all, that's what Hunter was—a normal person and a fellow grown up.

The only problem was, when Hunter climbed out of his car and jogged the few steps to the diner's door, he looked so handsome and fresh in his uniform—and so rugged...

Had she noticed that about him before? Just how was Kari going to behave her grown self now?

Chapter 9
Hunter

Because of the unexpected events surrounding the death of Lila Baldwin, Hunter stayed up much later than expected, and that he preferred the previous night. The paperwork had taken him well into the wee hours of the morning, but he wouldn't have missed this breakfast with Kari Sweet for the world.

He worried that if he had cancelled, Kari might never agree to another date. The timing was perfect when he asked, and such circumstances might never align again.

A second reason was that he very much wanted to know how she was holding up. After all, discovering a dead body when you were a cop was one thing, but, for a civilian, when that body belonged to a friend? That was another thing altogether.

He had powered through his early morning run that morning, taking the shorter route so he could get to the diner on time.

Inadvertently discovering Lila's body must have been a horrible experience for Kari and Kasi. Hunter hoped he could provide Kari with some measure of comfort. As he jogged toward the diner, he spotted Kari already waiting for him, sitting by the window.

He couldn't help but think that was a good sign. She was already waiting for him, so she must feel the same way. He also didn't fail to notice that she looked stunning with her hair pulled up like that–even if she might well have had a fretful and disturbed night.

He had always loved the way she looked. Kari Sweet was tall, beautiful, and had a headful of silky curls that he wanted to run his hands through.

Of course, those bright green eyes really were her best feature. So unusual and so striking – Hunter never failed to notice them whenever they met.

Hunter had had a crush on Kari since their high school days. Back then, he'd been seriously skinny. His teenage self was gangly, uncoordinated, and, at the time, it had felt like he'd stay that way forever.

She had always been nice to him because that's who she was, but he'd known he wouldn't have stood a chance then, even if he'd had the courage to ask her out on an actual date. Now though, he knew he was in great shape, and he knew as well that Kari Sweet definitely took notice whenever he turned up in On Bitter Grounds.

Hunter pushed the door of the diner open and dropped his shoulders back a little. Heading straight to the table where Kari was sitting, he was about to take a seat and greet his date when Nikki came over to take his order—a little too enthusiastically for his liking.

He knew full well that Nikki would say yes in a heartbeat if he was to ask her out, but she was too young and immature for him. After a painful teen phase, it seemed like he had his pick now. He enjoyed his newfound popularity with women. Hunter knew there were a few women around town who would agree if he asked them out.

But, he also knew there was really only one woman in his sights. Kari Sweet was the one he wanted, the one he'd always wanted really.

Drawing Nikki's attention back to his companion at the table, Hunter took his seat smiling, embarrassed at Nikki's obvious attentiveness.

"Are you ready to order, Kari?" he asked trying to bring the focus to her.

"Yes, I am, thank you. I'll take blueberry pancakes and a side of sausage please, Nikki."

"Good choice," he replied as he checked out the menu. "I'll take a country boy breakfast with scrambled eggs, sausage, biscuit, hash brown casserole, and two fluffy buttermilk pancakes. Oh, and a glass of orange juice, too." He added on seeing the refreshing glass of juice in front of Kari.

"So, now I've had a chance to sit down, I get the chance to say hello properly!" he said, smiling.

"Good morning, Hunter," Kari replied with a twinkle in her eye.

"Good morning, Kari, your breakfast order sounded good," he said. He was glad she wasn't one of those girls who pretended not to be hungry and was too afraid to order real food on a date.

He liked that she was secure in herself and that she knew what she wanted. That was definitely one of her many attractive qualities.

He paused a moment before asking his next question, "How are you doing?" he asked gently, referring to the terrible events of the previous evening.

"I don't know, I guess it honestly hasn't hit me that she's really gone," Kari replied sadly.

Hunter nodded in recognition. He remembered all too well the first time he had lost someone close to him, and the time it had taken for their absence to really sink in for him and to realize that they weren't coming back.

He hoped that she could handle it once the newness of the previous night has worn off and she was left with a gaping hole where her friend had been. The shock brought about by an untimely death wasn't something easy to get over, or to forget.

"I get it, it's never easy to lose someone you knew well. And how is Kasi holding up?"

"I really don't know. We didn't talk about it last night and I didn't see her this morning before I left. I guess we'll talk more about it when we get home from the shop this evening. I don't think we'll have the chance today – not if yesterday's anything to go by. We'd been busy with the store," Kari answered before continuing, "Do you have any idea who could have been responsible? Who could have done such a terrible thing?"

"Well, I'm not really supposed to comment on an open investigation. But seeing as you and Kasi were the ones who found her, I can tell you that we don't have any leads yet. We're working on it, so don't worry. In a small town like this, we can't have bad people like that running around. We'll catch them."

He could tell by the forlorn look on her face that he hadn't made her feel any better. He understood too well that anything as out of place and violent as the murder of someone in a close community, like the one in Mills Township, was going to scare everyone, especially the person who discovered the body.

Everyone back at the station was a little shaken, too. Things like this didn't just happen in a small town like theirs.

He decided to change the subject, and elected to ask her on her and Kasi's recent trip to the Food and Retail Expo in Chicago. That will surely take her mind off Lila's murder.

"Hey, so how did the expo go? In Chicago, right?"

"Oh, it was great! We've had a ton of orders since we came back so we must've done something right. It was really worth going as it seems to have really helped the business out. I've never been so glued to my computer before!" she answered, glad to talk about something so positive, rather than be reminded of Lila again.

Before they knew it, their food arrived, and both Hunter and Kari tucked into their breakfast meals, enjoying every bite of their delicious food. They spent nearly an hour as they chatted and ate, enjoying each other's company as much as the food on their plates. Kari couldn't remember the last time she had taken the time to sit down and actually enjoy her breakfast.

Hunter checked his watch and was surprised by how much time had passed.

"I have to go or I'll be late for work."

Kari checked her watch as well and was equally surprised, "Me, too! Kasi will be run off her feet prepping everything all by herself!"

"Hey, I'll stop by later to see you and check how you're doing."

"That would be really nice, Hunter. Are you sure, though? Aren't you in for a crazy day at work?" Kari replied, worried that he might be in for a long day after the events of last night.

"No problem at all, I promise. Hey, let me get that." He said as Nikki gave them the bill.

"No way, let's split it," said Kari, pulling out her purse.

"No, this time is on me. I asked you out, remember?" Hunter said as he handed out a stack of bills to pay their check.

"If you insist, Hunter." Kari said appreciatively.

"I do, I do insist. Objection overruled," he said teasingly as he ushered her out to their waiting cars.

Chapter 10

Kari

Kari was surprised to find a parking spot only a block away from the shop. By this hour, the streets were usually busy as residents and shopkeepers started their days.

So, finding a parking spot near On Bitter Grounds could be difficult, especially when the weather wasn't great. Nobody wanted to have to walk any further than absolutely necessary.

Fortunately for Kari, somebody must have just left their spot. This was a relief because she was hoping to get to work as soon as possible. Her breakfast date with Hunter had gone well, but it also lasted longer than she'd expected. Though she was glad they had so much to talk about, she felt guilty that she left her sister at the shop alone.

Kari parked her Jeep and jogged to the shop, wondering how Kasi was handling their usual morning rush. She definitely owed her one for picking up the slack. The shop had been busier than ever, and it had almost become too much for the two of them to handle.

It definitely wasn't a job for one person, even if that person was as energetic as her sister. She knew that

Kasi was also probably tired from lack of sleep the night before and would be more stressed than usual.

I should have just rescheduled breakfast, Kari thought. Hunter would have understood.

Kari flung open the front door of the shop and noticed a line was already forming. Many of the customers were regulars, so she gave them a wave and a smile. Kari assumed some of them were probably wondering why she was getting there so late as she was usually there to open the shop with her sister.

Let them wonder, she thought. I just need to get them their coffees ASAP.

Kari apologized to everyone in line as she quickly made her way behind the counter, making eye contact with her sister as she did so. The look in Kasi's eyes was one of relief, more than anger. It seemed like Kari had arrived just in a time as Kasi was clearly close to losing her cool.

Kari swiftly put on her apron and washed her hands, ready to dive into work. The Sweet sisters had a little bit of a backlog to get through, but they would manage. They always did.

Kari immediately started taking orders and grinding coffee beans. She tried her best to take on the bulk of the work since Kasi had to do so much by herself earlier. The sisters were a well-oiled machine, and they were able to keep people from waiting too long for their orders.

She knew that her regulars were willing to give her a break every once in a while—especially for coffee as good as theirs.

It took a little while, but eventually things calmed down a bit. Some customers got their coffee and pastries and headed off to work while a few hung around the shop to enjoy their purchases and chat.

The sisters loved watching their happy customers enjoy their coffee and each other's company. It was definitely one of the best parts of the job.

As the remaining customers finished their drinks and left, the sisters finally had a chance to talk for the first time that morning. Kari turned to her sister Kasi, who breathed a huge sigh of relief.

"We made it," Kasi said.

"Sorry, I ran a little late, I got over here as soon as I could," Kari replied.

"Don't sweat it. I was prepared for that to happen. Although, even with my preparation, I was starting to feel the heat before you got here," Kasi remarked.

"You handled it really well. Thank you for covering for me," Kari took a sip of her own coffee. "Did you sleep as badly as I did last night?"

"I slept terribly," Kasi confirmed. "It's a good thing we make coffee for a living because I really needed some this morning." She gave her sister the once-over, her eyes lingering on Kari's chignon. "At least your hair looks great even if you have racoon eyes."

Kari gave her sister a little playful punch in the arm. "Well, Hunter didn't seem to mind," she said with a laugh.

Kasi laughed as well and playfully punched her sister back. "I was just teasing you. You still look great. Even when you're exhausted, you look gorgeous."

"Maybe I should try a mohawk then. What do you think of that?" Kari joked. "I bet I could pull it off."

"Go for it. I'm sure our customers will love it. Just be sure to dye it purple too."

Since they had a little time, the sisters began preparing for lunch. It was business as usual as they made the changes and alterations for the switch from morning to afternoon customers. The coffee remained the same, but the food items were different.

As they worked, the sisters avoided discussing Lila Baldwin's murder and instead focused on how Kari's breakfast date with Hunter went.

"It went really well," Kari told her with a smile. "Hunter asked about you. He was wondering how you're doing after last night."

"Did you tell him I'm a mess?" Kasi replied.

Though she said it as a joke, Kari worried there was some truth behind her question. Kari and Kasi had just undergone a terrible experience. It would've been bad enough for them to find out Lila had been murdered, seeing and discovering the body was even worse.

"It's so crazy that Lila was murdered. I can't believe she's gone," Kari said. "It's okay if you're a mess. I am, too."

"Thanks, sis." Kasi blew out a long breath and shook her head. "How were Jenna and Laura so calm about this stuff? They found lots of dead bodies and, instead of being freaked out, they tried to help find the killer! We found one dead body and I feel like I'm going to be sick every time I think about it."

"I do, too," Kari agreed. "I don't know how long it will be until I feel normal again. Maybe we should call Jenna or Laura tonight. They might have some good insight on dealing with something like this."

"That's a good idea," Kasi replied.

The Sweet sisters already had a plan, but they also had a job to do. The coffee shop still had customers, and they still had to make them coffee and lunch. The world didn't stop spinning, so Kari and Kasi had to put on a brave face and press on.

Customers kept coming in, and many of them offered their condolences to the sisters. It was a small town, and a lot of people knew how close Kari and Kasi were to Lila. Each time, the sisters would give a quiet thanks, and then take the customer's order.

Morning turned to afternoon, and breakfast turned to lunch. Their special of the day was vegetable soup that they had made themselves in the shop. Soup was always a good idea when the weather was bad. Their customers enjoyed having something to warm them up.

Since the shop was not equipped with a full kitchen, the Sweet sisters usually tried to make vegetarian options to cut down on prep time and waste.

As the lunch crowd lined up, order after order came in for the soup and the girls were glad it was a hit. Between the weather, the grief and uncertainty about Lila's death, it seemed a cup of comfort food was just what the doctor ordered.

Kari and Kasi might not solve murders like their friends in Hartfell Cove, but they could at least make sure everyone in town was well-fed and caffeinated during the investigation.

Chapter 11

Kari

The afternoon sun was shining above On Bitter Grounds, and the popular coffee shop continued to buzz with activity. The tables were all filled with both the shop's regulars and other locals looking for refuge from the chilly midday air, leaving the Sweet sisters frazzled as usual with long lines and complicated coffee orders.

It was a constantly hectic setup, but Kari never really minded. She loved managing the coffee shop and all their customers, who were almost always warm and friendly. As a small business owner, she could not ask for more.

And of course, the coffee shop bustle kept her mind off her friend's untimely death.

"Here ya go, Mr. Martinez, one extra special caramel macchiato with a side of vegetable soup," she said, handing a middle-aged man in a suit his favorite order.

"Thanks Kari, I could really use something sweet and savory today," he replied. "This weather can have such a negative effect on your day."

He then looked at Kari with worry on his face. "I hope you girls are doing okay after what happened to Lila."

In a small town like Mills Township, everyone knows about each other's close relationships. All day long, customers have been comforting both her and Kasi about Lila's death.

"Oh, don't worry about us, Mr. Martinez. We're strong enough to handle ourselves and keep this entire ship going. It will take a lot to bring me and my sister down," she responded, trying to brush off her own anxieties and put on a happy face.

"I'm glad to hear it," he said, smiling at Kari as he took his tray to an empty table.

After a while, things slowed. With no new customers coming in, Kari took advantage of the rare moment of calm by checking on Kasi, who was busy running back and forth between roasting coffee beans and catering to online orders.

Feeling playful and forgetting her troubles for a moment, she snuck behind her sister who was hunched in front of a computer.

"Boo!"

Kasi was slightly off-balanced on her swivel chair and cried, "Kari, I swear on a bowl of vegetable soup—if you don't stop scaring me, I'm gonna record you singing in the shower and send it to Hunter."

Kari laughed, and the sound of her sister's humor put Kasi instantly at ease. She was glad she was able to lighten the mood.

"Still won't stop me. Your squeals of surprise have always been priceless," Kari said. She put both her hands on Kasi's shoulders and looked at the monitor. "So, how are things holding up here?"

"I just processed a large order for a bar mitzvah in Pennsylvania. Apparently, the kid really likes coffee. Can you believe that?"

"If it's our coffee, I don't blame him. Let's give the finest that Mills Township has to offer."

Kari heard the bell ring and turned her head to check on the people coming in. She saw a gaggle of college-age girls lining up in front of the counter. "There's my cue!" she told her sister. "Can't keep the people waiting for their caffeine."

***

Kari picked up a broom as the last of their customers, a group of senior citizens on a night out, left the shop.

Kasi cleaned up their table and headed back to the stockroom to check on supplies.

Finally, the two sisters were afforded some silence. The busy nature of the coffee shop provided a welcome distraction from their thoughts, but now they were faced with the emotion of what they were going through.

"It feels surreal, don't you think?" Kasi asked.

"What is?"

"Lila's murder. I mean, how things seemed to change because of it."

"How so?"

"Well, I just don't see the town in the same light as before. Now it just seems…full of secrets and stuff," Kasi said as she pulled a bag of coffee beans from the stock room.

"I just can't stop thinking about the murder," she continued, heaving a sigh as she pulled the heavy bag to one side. "Suddenly, Mills Township isn't so idyllic anymore. The fact that Lila was so close to us makes it even worse. A local murder is one thing, but the murder of someone you've always looked up to as a mentor is another."

As Kasi's mood turned somber, Kari felt hers follow suit. She'd always been sensitive to her sister's moods and was lucky that Kasi was usually incredibly upbeat and positive. When she's upset, though, it usually rubs off on Kari as well.

"I know. I just can't figure out why someone would want to kill her. She was always so nice to us and I saw her being nice to every client whenever we drop by her shop..."

"You know, I wish Jenna and Laura were here to help us. I hope they can talk when we call them later," Kasi said, her seriousness finally fading away. She was smiling as she was refilling the sugars and creams.

"Oh yeah, I know what you mean. Those ladies must have some good advice on situations such as this! I wonder how they're doing," Kari replied. She remembered how she and Kasi clicked instantly with the two women and the stories Jenna and Laura told them whenever they had opportunities to chase criminals.

"I wonder if they're still wrapped up in solving murders back home," Kasi joked, reading her mind as usual. "Plus, I really miss them. I never would have thought we'd get a chance to travel so far from home and make new friends, especially ones like them."

They finished putting the shop in order for the next day and were preparing to leave. After wiping off a few stains, Kasi sat on one of the tables and looked wistfully out the large windows.

"Hey, what's wrong?" Kari asked.

"It could've been us."

"What do you mean?" Kari felt her heart speed up.

"It could've been us who were killed in Style Factory. We could've been killed just as easily in that shop."

Kari sat beside Kasi and put her hand on her sister's shoulder. Her sister's remarks made her uneasy, but she knew she had to be the big sister in this situation and make her feel better.

"I know that we're used to this being a town where nothing bad ever happens," she told Kasi. "But the world is changing. It doesn't mean we're not safe anymore. It just means we have to adjust; maybe double check that our doors are locked at night and carry some pepper spray? It's not a bad idea."

"You're right," Kasi agreed with a sigh. "We should take it as a sign, warning us to be more careful."

"Let's not worry too much about it, okay, sis? It's not good for the coffee." Kari's joke was an attempt to lighten the mood, but it fell flat.

"It's just scary, okay?" Kasi replied. "I know you're right, but it still bothers me."

"Well, I think for now it's best to stay vigilant. We still don't know why Lila was killed, but we should be prepared. Until the psycho is caught, we have to make sure that we're never alone anywhere, deal?" Kari's voice was full of a confidence she didn't really feel. "I'm sorry if you felt like I was blowing off your fear."

"Deal. Now let's go home where I can finally relax with a steaming mug of hot chocolate," Kasi stood up from the table and put the mops away in the closet, her final job of the day. Kari turned off the rest of the shop's machines and all of the lights, and the pair locked up for the evening.

Kari's Jeep was only a few steps away, but, for the sisters, it felt like miles. She had been thinking about Lila's killer, and how he or she could jump out at any moment. The gravity of the murder was finally settling in.

I really hope the killer is not in the backseat, Kari caught herself thinking. She brushed the thought off. Maybe I've been watching too many horror movies lately.

Kasi kept looking over her shoulder as well, her eyes seemingly unable to focus on a straight direction. Once again, an air of uneasiness was hanging above the sisters' heads, and Kari didn't like it one bit.

Even in the confines of the Jeep, the looming anxiety was impossible to shake off. Kari could tell it was going to be a long ride home. She sighed quietly as she turned the key and started the car.

I just want my safe and happy Mills Township back to how it was, she thought. But as with everything else in life, change had happened and there was nothing she could do but accept it.

Chapter 12

Kari

Kari and Kasi arrived at their charming house and parked.

"Let's go!" Kari yelled.

They rushed from the car to the house, but not because of the chilly weather. Unfortunately, fear had a grip on the sisters. The moment they were inside, they slammed and locked the door shut, making sure the lock's working properly.

The murder of Lila Baldwin had hit them hard and changed their view of the quaint town they had grown up in.

I can't let my guard down for even a millisecond, Kari thought, I must be wary and keep safe and protect my sister.

The Sweet girls looked at each other knowingly. They can convey so much to one another with just a simple glance. Not only were they afraid but they were also sad that this was going to be their reality until the murderer was caught.

Now that they were safely inside their home, they could relax a bit at least. Some normalcy was necessary after all.

"Hey, did you get a chance to eat anything today after breakfast?" Kasi asked.

"Not really. I nibbled on something at the coffee shop around lunchtime, but we were just so busy today. I couldn't find the time to eat with the crowd we had," Kari replied.

Holding her stomach, the younger Sweet sister remarked, "I didn't even get to do that, and I didn't have breakfast either. I'm absolutely starving. I'll make us something,"

"You don't have to do that. I can just eat an apple or something," Kari countered.

Kasi dismissed this notion with a wave of her hand. "That's ridiculous. I have to make something for myself, so I'll make you something, too. Don't worry about it. Just keep me company in the kitchen."

Kari agreed to these terms and followed her younger sister into the kitchen. She watched as Kasi went into food preparation mode, heading into the fridge and grabbing some shredded chicken and mayonnaise. This meant chicken salad was on the menu.

Kasi worked with such precision that Kari believed this is how she copes with fear and stress. It was a good idea to lose yourself in some mundane task. Just getting lost in the thought of her sister cooking has already made her feel a little bit better.

Man, it looks so good, Kari thought.

With the salad ready, Kasi grabbed a couple of flaky croissants and cut them in half. She then popped them into the toaster for a few seconds, just to warm them a bit. Once the halves shot back up, Kasi grabbed them and, in one fluid motion, placed them on two plates.

Finishing the dish, Kasi picked one up and presented it to her sister with a big smile.

She was so thankful to have a sister like Kasi. Kari loved that they got to live and work together. Sure, it meant they had to see each other pretty much all the time, but the sisters rarely got on each other's nerves. Kari was baffled by those families where nobody hangs out or talks; she loved having her sister around.

Gosh, what would I do without her?

Of course, she also loved that Kasi watched cooking shows all the time and liked to try out new recipes. She was definitely the one with the magic touch when it came to food. As long as Kari had her sister around, she knew that there was also a tasty meal on the horizon.

"You've done it again, sis." Kari said after just one bite of her sandwich. "It's absolutely delicious."

"Thanks," Kasi replied with a smile.

With that, the two sisters headed into the living room and plopped down on the couch to finish eating. They chose a cooking show on TV and chowed down their chicken salad sandwiches.

The sisters ate in silence as neither one could stop eating long enough to form a coherent sentence. In a matter of minutes, both sandwiches were reduced to crumbs.

Looking at each other's empty plates, they shared a much needed laugh. It felt good to have a nice moment together after all the stress they felt on their drive home.

"You know, maybe we should try calling Jenna and Laura right now," Kari suggested.

"I agree. Now that I have some food in me, I feel a bit better, and I've wanted to talk to those two all day. I miss them."

"I miss them, too. Plus, if anybody can help us deal with…everything that's happened, it's them. They're in the same time zone, so they've probably gotten off work by now," Kari said.

Kasi grabbed her phone and began tapping the screen.

"I'm going to text Laura to make sure she's available to talk."

Kari followed her sister's lead in getting her phone out.

"I'll text Jenna, then."

It took a few minutes, but both the ladies from Hartfell Cove texted back to say they were free and had planned on getting together shortly.

A short time later, Jenna texted again and said that they were ready to talk. Kari placed the call and put the phone on speaker so her sister could hear as well.

"Hello?" Jenna's voice rang out through the phone.

"Jenna! It's Kari! Gosh, it's so good to hear your voice!"

"It's great to hear from you, too. I'm so glad that you, ladies, wanted to talk today. Oh, Laura's also here. Say hello, Laura."

"I just want to let you know Jenna isn't my boss and I don't do whatever she tells me to do. Still, I want to say hi, but remember it's my choice, not Jenna's."

The sisters both laughed. They loved the rapport that Jenna and Laura had. It reminded them of their own relationship. They regarded one another as sisters although they weren't even related.

"Hi, you two, this is Kasi. I hope you can tell my voice from Kari's over the phone."

The four women spent some time catching up on events from the time they met at the Food and Retail Expo in Chicago. It was also where Kari and Kasi found out about their new pals' history of investigating murders. To the Sweet sisters, the girls from Maine had the craziest lives, but they were also fascinating people.

They also excitedly shared recent success stories on their businesses.

"Jenna, I'm going to send you an order for biscotti soon!" Kari noted.

The happiness in Jenna's voice was clear when she said, "That's great! I can't wait to bake them!"

"We also thought that your coffee-scented candles would be a great addition to the gift baskets we sell. Do you think you're ready for an order, Laura?" Kasi inquired.

The conversation was fun and lively, but Kari knew they had to get down to more serious business.

"Hey, guys, it's been great catching up with you, two. But Kasi and I really needed to talk to you about something a little more pressing. Do you mind?"

"Oh, this sounds serious! Of course, we have time!" Jenna exclaimed.

"Well, something terrible happened in town recently. And, to be honest, Kasi and I have been having trouble dealing with it, but we thought you and Laura could help us out."

The sisters took turns filling their friends in on everything that happened. They recounted how they had been walking by Lila's boutique when they saw a shadowy figure moving around. Never thinking that something was wrong, they entered the shop only to find their friend and mentor murdered.

"As if that wasn't enough," Kari said, "Now we're afraid, and we just don't know how to handle all of these."

"Wow, that's awful. I understand why you called. Unfortunately, I have a lot of history with dead bodies, so I guess I've become an expert, to a degree. Here's what I think you should do…"Jenna said.

It wasn't long before Kari and Kasi felt truly relaxed. The suggestions made by their friends were a tremendous help.

"Thank you so much. I think both Kasi and I feel a lot better— at least I do." Kari said.

"No problem. Feel free to call anytime. Good luck," Jenna said.

"Thanks. We'll let you know how things turn out," Kari replied.

The sisters said goodbye to their friends and ended the call. They looked at each other with a real sense of relief.

"So, where do we begin?" Kasi asked her sister.

Chapter 13

Hunter

Hunter let out a big yawn as he sat at his desk and didn't even bother to try and stifle it.

"God, I'm so tired," he said, running a hand through his hair. It was late, and Hunter was burning the candle at both ends. "This is what happens on murder cases," he told himself, "especially your first one."

Since he was practically alone, he could get away with talking to himself.

Hunter was pulling another all-nighter, investigating the Lila Baldwin case, which had consumed pretty much the entire police department since it happened. It was, by a wide margin, the biggest case they had faced in the recorded history of the town. This wasn't the first late night Hunter had faced since Lila was murdered, and he knew it wouldn't be the last.

"I should've just hit the snooze instead of going for a run this morning," he muttered.

The idea of getting a few minutes of extra sleep seemed so enticing as he struggled to get out of bed. However, he'd thought better of it. Running would give him a chance to burn off all the nervous energy and stress that had been building up inside him.

If he didn't go for a run, he knew he wouldn't be able to concentrate at work. Of course, it was also hard to concentrate when you're tired. That's where all the coffee came in.

"Thank god for On Bitter Grounds," he remarked, looking down at his large, empty cups that had once contained a delicious dark roast.

Hunter had made multiple trips over to the Sweets' coffee house that day, and the caffeine had given him a temporary energy boost that helped him through most of the evening.

Sure, we have coffee here, he thought to himself as he looked over at the station's pot, but I'm not sure it can even be called coffee. It was nasty, bitter brown water.

He also had to admit that he was going to On Bitter Grounds to see Kari just as much as he was going for the coffee. He had been able to see her a lot more often while working the Lila Baldwin case, which was one of the only perks.

But I still want to solve this as quickly as possible, he thought. A woman was murdered, after all.

I do enjoy seeing Kari more, though, he admitted to himself. Hopefully when the investigation's over, we can start seeing each other outside the coffee shop more. Maybe another breakfast date will be in the cards.

Not that Hunter imagined himself having time for a breakfast date—or any date anytime soon. He was spending pretty much every waking moment working.

He looked down at the Lila Baldwin case file in front of him. It had been growing slowly but surely as the investigation continued.

"I should take another look at this. Make sure I didn't miss anything," he said hopefully.

Unfortunately, there were no smoking guns or new key pieces of evidence in what he could see. He read the autopsy report once more.

"Nothing odd here…other than somebody from Mills Township being murdered,"

As far as murders went, it seemed pretty straightforward. She had seemingly been stabbed in the stomach, and that was what killed her. There was nothing about the wound that seemed odd.

The fingerprint evidence was not helpful in this instance either as well. Oh, they found fingerprints at the scene of the crime, and they weren't all Lila's. They were good prints, too.

The problem wasn't the quality of the fingerprints, but with the database the police department had. Either the killer had never been arrested before, or the database wasn't as up-to-date as Hunter would have liked.

People were in and out of the store during the day. Even if we found a match, that wouldn't guarantee we had the killer.

Hunter closed the file abruptly and pushed it across the desk. Frustration was building inside him. He took one of his coffee cups from On Bitter Grounds and angrily threw it at his trash can.

The cup missed, so he grabbed another empty cup and whipped it with all his might.

"That made me feel a little better at least," he said with a heavy sigh.

The case was at a dead end. The town was in an uproar over Lila Baldwin's murder, and Hunter could feel the sadness and fear whenever he went. He was especially aware of how torn up Kari and Kasi were about it since they'd been close to the victim.

When we figure this out, the town will feel like itself again, Hunter told himself. It had to.

He got out of his seat and walked toward a large whiteboard in the office. To this point, the whiteboard hadn't been used a ton by the station. Occasionally, a reminder would be written on it, but it was never really used for police work.

Now, it had been dubbed the 'murder board' and was dedicated to the investigation of Lila Baldwin's death.

"I never thought we'd have a murder board," Hunter said to nobody in particular. "Hopefully after this, it will go back to a plain old reminder board."

He looked at the board, which had a few scattered notes on it but nothing very helpful.

"All we need now is a suspect and some evidence," he said indignantly.

The only people with any connection to Lila's murder were Kari and Kasi, and that was only because they had found the body. They weren't suspects, though, as they had been ruled out the night of the murder.

Hunter stared at the board and once again felt how surreal this case was. Mills Township was a safe place to live. At worst, there had been a couple of break-ins here and there, with stores being robbed after they were closed.

Usually, though, the issues were minor and consisted of vandalism or public drunkenness. Stuff that was easy to handle, stuff that was cut and dry. There was rarely any mystery to solve, so a ton of detective work was never needed.

The idea of having to visualize a timeline for a crime was new to everybody at the station.

For a murder like this, though, such a timeline was needed. Hunter picked up a dry erase marker and approached the board. He drew a long horizontal line across the board.

Then, he went to the far right and drew a little notch extending about two inches. Above that vertical line he wrote 'LILA MURDERED' in big block letters.

"Alright, Lila," he said to the deceased woman, "let's try and figure out what happened to you."

Thanks to the autopsy, Hunter had an idea when Lila had been murdered. This was good, because otherwise they would have to guess based on when the body was found, which was less reliable. If they knew when she was killed, they could better verify alibis.

Hopefully, by establishing a timeline, I can shake some suspects out, Hunter thought.

He began filling in all the information on the timeline prior to the murder. They had some info on when people had last seen her, though none of it seemed terribly helpful. However, everything needed to be recorded, as it might become important later.

After writing all the info on the timeline and adding some more intel on the whiteboard, Hunter took a step back.

"It's a start," he told himself. "We're going to figure this out, Lila. The information is out there."

The whiteboard was on wheels, so Hunter decided to move it into the conference room. There, it would take up less space but still be readily available to everybody on the force.

If anybody else got a new lead or a new piece of evidence, they could go into the conference room and add it. That way, they could all work together, and hopefully as a group find Lila's murderer.

After moving the whiteboard, Hunter looked at his watch. It was already past eleven o'clock. His eyes widened.

"Geez, I've been working for twelve hours straight with no break." he said with a sigh. "I should go home."

Though Hunter hated to admit defeat, he needed to get some sleep. By the time he got home and to his bed, he'd only have a few hours before he had to get up and come to work all over again.

I might miss my run tomorrow morning, he thought.

As he gathered his stuff to leave, a thought occurred to him.

Tomorrow, I'll get to see Kari when I buy my coffee. I'll probably see her a few times, actually.

Maybe that made the late nights worth it in the end.

Chapter 14

Kari

"How'd you sleep last night?" Kari asked her sister as she checked for online orders the next morning.

They'd arrived at the shop about half an hour before it was time to open, giving them some time to chat before the morning rush.

"Not great," Kasi admitted, "but better than the other night when I couldn't sleep at all. I, at least, won't be totally dead on my feet today. How about you? Given how your hair looks this morning, I imagine you slept better."

Kari patted her curly locks, which she had time to put up into a couple of French braids. "I slept okay. Talking to Jenna and Laura helped a bit, I think."

"I totally agree," Kasi said, finishing up the online orders and moving to the latte machine.

"I'm so glad we decided to call them. I'm also glad we decided to feature these mocha lattes. They're a hit!"

Kari nodded. She was just as happy as her sister that their special was making an impact on the customers, but it had been difficult for her to concentrate on work since Lila's death. Speaking with Jenna and Laura, who were veterans at this sort of thing, had made her feel less like their quaint little world was coming to an end.

"There probably isn't a deranged killer running around town murdering people willy-nilly. It's probably somebody who knew the victim and had an axe to grind," Jenna had told the sisters when they'd spoken on the phone.

"You really think it's someone who had a personal grudge against Lila like Jenna suggested?" Kari asked her sister.

Kasi shrugged. "It seems logical, though I'm still having trouble figuring out who that might be. It does seem a lot more likely that a homicidal maniac killed her for no reason, especially since there haven't been any more deaths."

Kari shuddered at the words more deaths. How in the world would they be dealing with this if more people had been killed? She couldn't even imagine.

"Jenna suggested we find the person with the grudge, and then we'd find the killer," Kari reminded her. "But what happens if we can't find anyone with a grudge?"

"There has to be someone," Kasi insisted. "No matter how well-liked she was, I'm sure she had upset someone along the way. We just have to keep looking and asking questions."

Do I really want to try and figure out who killed Lila? Kari wondered. Are we really up for that?

After talking it over with her sister, they decided that they could be involved in the case without being too involved in the case.

"We can try and solve the case without actually trying to catch the killer," Kasi suggested. "Then, we can just tell Hunter what we know, and he can make the arrest."

Kari nodded. "I agree. We have access to a lot of people who come through the shop. We just need to keep our ears open."

However, once the morning rush started, they found they were so busy that listening for clues was the last thing on their mind. With the chilly weather and many people grieving over Lila's death, warm coffee and gooey treats were on top of their lists. On Bitter Grounds was crowded until mid-morning when the girls finally got a bit of a break.

Knowing they would only have a few minutes before the lunch rush started, the sisters took a moment to talk.

"Can you think of anybody that might have wanted to hurt Lila? Anybody from her life that might have a grudge?" Kasi asked.

"Lila had never been married and had no kids," Kari noted. "So that rules out an ex-husband or a baby daddy."

Kasi nodded in agreement before adding, "And she wasn't dating anybody seriously. What if she was having an affair with somebody, though? Maybe she was the other woman in a love triangle?"

"That could be a reason for somebody to want to harm Lila," Kari admitted.

The sisters had barely made any headway when they heard the bell over the door ring, which meant a new customer was coming in. Kari looked up at the clock.

"Oh, it's about time for the lunch rush," she remarked.

Kasi nodded, and both girls got up from their seats. They couldn't relax any longer because a bunch of folks were about to pile through the front door. Just as anticipated, the lull quickly became a rush, and the girls were once again swamped with customers.

Kari was doling out coffee and sandwiches as quickly as possible, her mind racing to keep up with the next order, when she spotted a familiar face. Hunter was in line. She felt a smile spread across her face when their eyes met.

Isn't this his second visit today? she thought. Not that she was complaining.

"What can I get you?" Kari asked him when it was his turn to order.

"My usual large dark roast with a touch of cream," he told her with a grin. "Oh, and also one of those chicken salad croissants you've got as your special today. That sounds good."

"It is," Kari told him. "Trust me."

The chicken salad croissants were tangy and meaty with plenty of celery, almonds, and bits of cranberry. Kasi had been trying variations of her salad for months, and this newest offering was definitely her best. The customers at the shop seemed to agree as they had received rave reviews.

"Wow! That is so good," Hunter complimented after taking a bite. "You weren't kidding!"

"Told ya," Kari replied with a smile.

Since the Lila Baldwin case was on her mind, she decided to take this opportunity to ask Hunter for some information. Maybe it would help her think of suspects.

"So, Hunter, how's the case going?"

She saw Hunter sigh at the question.

"Not great," he admitted. "We don't have any suspects yet. We're working on it, though. We're doing everything we can to solve this."

"I'm sure you are," Kari assured. "Kasi and I are trying to rack our brains to come up with someone who might have a grudge against Lila, but we're having trouble."

Kasi must have overheard them, because she popped in with a question of her own. "Has anybody made arrangements for her funeral yet?"

"Lila has an aunt living in an assisted living facility around here," Hunter said. "She's making all the arrangements and paying for the entire thing."

"That's a relief," Kari said. "I'm glad Lila has a family member looking out for her."

"I wonder if she needs any help?" Kasi inquired. "I mean, if she's elderly…." She looked at her sister, who shrugged her shoulders.

"Well, ladies, I'm going to leave you to it," Hunter remarked after finishing his sandwich. "I have to get back to the station, see if we can pull any more clues out of the woodwork."

Kari and Kasi watched him go.

I can't believe there are still no suspects, Kari mused. *That's it. Kasi and I have to help, or this case is never going to get solved.*

Chapter 15

Kari

He really is wonderful. I just can't seem to stop smiling. I hope he doesn't get too mad at us for snooping a little, though.

After Hunter left On Bitter Grounds, there was an obvious spring in Kari's step as she went about her work. She was feeling pretty good after having her moment with Hunter. Even though Lila's murder investigation had come up in the conversation, it hadn't dampened Kari's spirits.

As she was working, Kari couldn't help noticing Kasi rolling her eyes. She knew her sister well enough to know that eye roll was meant for her.

"What is it?" Kari asked.

"Nothing. It's just that you and Hunter are so cute together," Kasi said with a sly smile.

"Oh, are we?"

"Yeah. You did realize that was his second time in the shop today, right? Do you think that's just about the coffee?" Kasi remarked.

Kari didn't retort to this. Instead, she just stuck her tongue out in response.

"Let's get back to work."

Kasi agreed, only because they had a lot of work to do. There was still a line for the lunch rush, and the sisters were hoping they would be able to sell out their chicken salad croissant sandwiches before it was over.

Such a huge success would be a testament to Kasi's touch when it came to creating tasty treats. Kari loved that her sister's skill with food gave their coffee shop a whole new dimension.

I really hit the jackpot with her.

The lunch rush ended, but a few more customers strolled in throughout the remainder of the day. The slow traffic wasn't a big deal, though, as the morning and early afternoon had been quite busy. Occasionally, some people would stream in after work, tired from a long day on the grind, but coffee sales tended to steadily decline as the day went on.

Fortunately, a couple of the afternoon customers decided to grab some chicken salad, which meant that the sisters indeed sold out their lunch special. Surely, they had to extend the offer after lunch, but it was still a big success.

The quieter hours gave Kari more time to think about Lila Baldwin. Her heart was still broken over the loss of her friend.

Why would anybody want to murder her?

Kari also remembered what Hunter said about Lila's aunt taking care of the funeral.

I'll have to find out when plans are finalized so Kasi and I can close the shop to go. Maybe we can pay Lila's aunt a visit and pay our respects a little early…

It still bothered Kari that there were no clear leads on Lila's case. This was a small town, and surely, the person responsible wouldn't be able to evade the police for much longer.

A scary thought occurred to her. What if the person who did this was just a drifter?

Kari wasn't sure if that was a more or less comforting thought than believing someone they knew could be a killer.

When the day came to a close, the girls counted down the register and started cleaning up. It was inevitable for drinks to get spilled a bit here and there, so the girls liked cleaning thoroughly before stains set in on the tile grout.

After On Bitter Grounds was nice and tidy, Kari and Kasi closed the shop for the day. They were both happy with how their day had unfolded.

"What do you want to do for dinner?" Kari asked her sister.

"I'm not sure. I don't really feel like cooking, if I were to be honest."

"And you probably don't want me cooking because I can't do it as well as you can," Kari joked.

"Yeah. After eating my own food, I can't imagine choking down something you made," Kasi replied with a laugh.

"We could go out to get something," Kari suggested.

"Hey! I got an idea!" Kasi excitedly said. "Why don't we go visit Mom and Dad? I bet we can have dinner over there."

"Oh, I like that idea a lot!" Kari agreed. "We haven't been over there in a couple of weeks. I'm sure they would love to see us, and we can use that to convince them to feed us."

The sisters were both excited to see their parents. They immediately prepared to leave and hopped into Kari's Jeep.

Their parents, Aaron and Nancy Sweet, lived about ten minutes from On Bitter Grounds, so it was an easy drive.

The street where they had grown up, Prairie Circle Way, might have different residents than the girls had grown up with. However, the neighborhood remained quite similar to how it had been when they were younger.

Kasi eyed the houses as Kari drove. She liked to notice any changes that had occurred.

When the subdivision was being built, the English Tudor style of house was in vogue, so the bulk of the homes on Prairie Circle Way were constructed in that fashion. The Sweets' home was no exception. There was a faux oldness to the whole thing, and even when the houses were large, they were designed to look like quaint, little cottages.

The Sweets' two-story house was dominated by herringbone brickwork, although the upper floor of the home was an alabaster white facing the street. There was also a great deal of lattice work and a brown thatched roof slightly darker than the tannish-brown that the rest of the house was.

Their home had several large windows as well, including one that belonged to Kasi as a kid. Kari's old bedroom was at the back of the house.

The sisters had spent their entire childhood living in this house. Kari had many wonderful memories of growing up on this street, playing outside with her sister and friends.

It was a great neighborhood, quiet and safe. Kids could play in the street without worrying about a car flying through.

I hope, someday, I can raise a family of my own in a neighborhood like this. Better yet, I'd love to see my children playing on the streets where I grew up, Kari wished.

I wonder if Hunter ever thinks about things like that. Wait, where did that thought come from?

The sisters pulled up into their parents' driveway and made their way to the front door. Kari knocked, and, soon thereafter, the door opened.

"Hi, Mom!" the sisters said in unison.

"Girls! What a great surprise!"

Mrs. Sweet called to her husband that their daughters were at the house. Aaron made his way to the door to greet both of his children with a hug.

"What brings you over?"

"Well, we were hoping to catch you before you had dinner," Kari answered.

"We were just talking about what to do for dinner tonight. Since you girls are here, how about I whip up some of my spaghetti and meatballs?" Nancy suggested.

"That would be amazing!" Kasi said delightedly.

"Oh, I've missed your spaghetti dinners!" Kari added.

"That settles it then," their mother replied.

The whole family made their way into the kitchen to talk while Nancy prepared dinner. Naturally, Kasi couldn't resist pitching in, while Kari and Aaron sat at the dinner table, waiting to be served. Fortunately, the kitchen led seamlessly into the dining room, allowing everybody to continue with their conversation.

"So, how's the coffee shop doing?" Nancy asked as she prepared the tomato sauce.

"Really good actually," Kari related. "We've been selling a ton of our roasted beans online, and today, our lunch special was sold out."

"That's great, honey," Nancy beamed.

"Yes, your mother and I are so proud of you two," Aaron added. "You've put so much work into that coffee house, and we're so happy it's paid off. You girls deserve it."

Soon enough, dinner was ready. Nancy served the main dish while Kasi brought over some garlic bread she had prepared to add a little crunch to the meal.

Mrs. Sweet's spaghetti and meatballs were somewhat famous in the neighborhood. Everybody agreed she made the best in town. That mostly came down to the sauce and the meatballs, as there were only so many ways to make spaghetti. She had a special touch, though.

Kari happily dug into the spaghetti. It was delicious.

"Oh, this is so good!" she exclaimed. "Why did we ever move out of the house when our mom is such a wonderful cook?"

"I know. We could be eating like this every night!" Kasi added.

"Well, Kari's bedroom doubles as my home office now, but if you two don't mind sharing a room and doing the dishes every night, maybe we can make that work," Aaron joked.

"Eh, maybe we're better off having our own place," Kari said with a smile.

Chapter 16

Kari

Kari and Kasi continued to happily chow down on their mom's spaghetti. It was the best dinner they had enjoyed in a while.

Kari took a bite out of the garlic bread that her sister had made. It was quite garlicky but still delicious.

"Good bread, sis," she said before she'd fully swallowed.

Now that the girls were adults, their parents no longer bothered to scold them for talking with their mouths full or putting their elbows on the table.

"Thanks," Kasi replied with a grin. "I put on extra cheese just for you."

"So how are you two holding up?" Aaron asked his daughters. "I mean, with the death of your friend Lila. I can't imagine finding your friend murdered."

Silence filled the room.

"Aaron, we're having dinner," Nancy told her husband gently. "Maybe now's not the best time to bring up murder."

"I'm sorry, hon," Aaron apologized. "But we haven't seen them since the…incident, and I'm worried about them. I can't help but ask."

"It's okay, Mom," Kari assured her. "We're doing alright. Well, I'm doing alright. I don't want to speak for Kasi."

"Yeah, I'm doing better now as well," Kasi said, giving both her parents a reassuring smile.

"We were afraid at first, thinking that there might be a crazy killer on the loose since we just couldn't imagine anybody wanting to kill Lila. Now, though, I'm less afraid and more upset that somebody would do that to someone as nice as Lila. We thought the world of her."

"I'm glad to hear you girls are doing okay," Aaron told his daughters. "I was worried you'd be afraid."

"So worried that I had to stop him from moving in with you girls until the killer was caught!" Nancy spoke up with an exasperated shake of her head. "I had to keep reminding him that you're adults now, and you don't really want your dad sleeping on the couch!"

Kari chuckled. "Well, at first, I'm not sure we would have turned him away. But then we talked to our friends Jenna and Laura. You remember the ones I told you about who we met in Chicago? Well, they've

117

been involved in quite a few investigations and have found a few dead bodies."

"My goodness!" Nancy exclaimed. "I can't even imagine."

"We asked them for some advice on how to handle this," Kari continued. "Jenna told us that it probably wasn't some deranged lunatic out there killing people randomly."

"Based on their experience," Kasi chimed in, "it's almost always somebody who was personally connected to the victim. She also said that if we found out who had a grudge against the victim, we'd probably find the killer. That's the easiest way to solve the case."

"I don't like hearing talk like that," Nancy said, her eyes narrowing. "Surely, you two aren't thinking about getting involved in solving the case? That would be so dangerous! Leave it to the police, girls. They know what they're doing."

Kari tried to calm her mother by saying, "No, don't worry, Mom. We have no desire to become detectives. We've only been trying to think of somebody for our own peace of mind. If we think of somebody who might have done it, we can pass that information along to the police."

"That's good," Aaron remarked, putting a hand on his wife's in a show of solidarity. "You two might be great coffee makers, but I don't know if you're cut out to be detectives."

"Yeah, we don't know the first thing about it," Kasi agreed. "All I know about being a detective is what I've seen on television. If it's not like being on Law & Order or Monk, I wouldn't have a clue. I wouldn't even know where to begin."

"When have you seen Monk?" Kari asked her sister. "Isn't that a little before your time?"

"They show reruns on some channel," Kasi explained. "I caught it once, and it was pretty good, so I tried to catch it again. I've only seen a few episodes, but it was one of the first things that came to mind when I thought of detectives."

"I always liked Columbo," Aaron said with a smile. "It might be dating me, but I thought that was a great show, and he was an amazing detective. I wish he was working the Lila Baldwin case."

Kari looked over at her mom and realized that she was squirming a bit in her seat, picking at her meatball but not eating it.

She knew that this was a bit of a sore subject with her parents. They didn't really want to talk about murder, and they certainly didn't want to hear about their daughters getting involved in any way in a murder case. Nancy, in particular, seemed like she was uncomfortable.

"Hunter came by the coffee house today," Kari shared, deciding that a change of subject was in order.

"That's Kari's boyfriend," Kasi noted teasingly.

"Oh?" Aaron asked, raising an eyebrow. "This is the first we've heard of a boyfriend!"

"He's not my boyfriend!" Kari defended, smacking her sister on the shoulder. "We went on one date!"

Kasi snickered into her napkin.

"Anyway," Kari continued, "Hunter told us that arrangements for Lila's funeral are being made by her aunt. Apparently, she's paying for the whole thing. Do either of you remember Lila's aunt at all? Hunter said that she's living in an assisted living facility now."

Both Aaron and Nancy were quiet for a second as they thought.

"I think I remember Lila having an aunt. She sounds familiar," Aaron recalled.

"I feel like her name was Clementine," Nancy noted.

"That's right!" Aaron snapped his fingers. "Clementine Fisher! I remember her now. I'm pretty sure that she was Lila's father's sister, if I recall correctly."

"Do you remember anything about her?" Kasi asked.

"Not a lot," Aaron admitted. "We certainly weren't close with Clementine. I believe she was married, but her husband died a few years ago."

"That's right. He had a heart attack," Nancy added.

"They didn't have any kids of their own, and I think Lila was sort of like a daughter to Clementine in that way," Aaron said.

"Aw, that's so sad. Clementine outlived both her husband her niece." Kasi frowned. "That would have been so hard."

As they finished up their dinner, the girls cleared the dishes, and Nancy offered up ice cream for dessert.

"Ugh, no, I'm stuffed," Kasi declined, rubbing her stomach. "That was so good!"

Kari declined dessert as well, and they all headed into the living room to relax. They put on a light sitcom, and all chuckled as the antics on the screen took their minds off the real-life events going on in their town.

After a while, Kari looked down at her watch to see what time it was. "I think Kasi and I need to head home soon," she announced. "We have to be up early, and I don't think either of us has been getting great sleep lately."

"Yeah, she's probably right," Kasi seconded.

Nancy and Aaron hugged both their daughters and told them they were welcome to come by anytime for dinner or just to talk.

"Keep us updated on what happens with Lila and Clementine," Nancy reminded as they gathered their things to leave. "And please, be careful."

The short drive home was quiet until Kasi suddenly said, "Hey, we have to go talk to the aunt, right?"

"About the funeral?" Kari clarified. "Or about the murder?"

"Both, I guess," Kasi answered with a shrug. "Maybe she would know if Lila had any enemies."

"Didn't we tell our parents we weren't going to play detective?" Kari asked, giving her sister a suspicious look.

"We're going to talk to an old woman in an assisted living facility," Kasi told her reasonably. "I don't think we're in any danger. Plus, I know you've been thinking the exact same thing."

"Duh," Kari said with a laugh.

"So, what's the plan?"

"How about tomorrow morning we call the place Clementine is in and see how late she can have guests?" Kari suggested.

"That sounds good. Do you know which facility it is?" Kasi inquired.

"The Behind the Pines Assisted Living Facility."

Both Kari and Kasi agreed on this plan and drove the rest of the way home in silence.

We'll finally get some answers tomorrow, Lila, Kari thought. The Sweet sisters are on the case.

Chapter 17

Kari

The two girls had spent the entire morning slaving away in the back room of On Bitter Grounds, trying to catch up.

Kari had been manning the roaster, while Kasi ran the packaging station. They had received a rush of online orders over the past few days and were struggling to keep up. Though the extra work was a little stressful, it kept their minds busy, and they both appreciated that.

Even though they had both agreed that they were going to talk to Lila's aunt, neither of them liked lying to their parents. Kari knew that their mom and dad were just worried because they cared, but this was their friend and mentor's murder they were talking about. She had been so good to them when they first decided to open the coffee house, and now they felt they had to do whatever they could to repay that favor.

Though Kari had no idea what they were actually going to do, talking to the aunt was at least a start.

The bell above the door rang, waking Kari from her thoughts.

"Oh, finally! Customers! You're on wrapping now, sis!" Kasi laughed as she went to the front door to help the customers who had just come in.

Kari finished roasting the batch that she was working on and took advantage of the cooling period to take a break.

She reached into her pocket and pulled out the small slip of paper with a phone number on it that she'd looked up that morning. From her other pocket, she took her cell phone. After taking a deep breath, she dialed the number and waited.

"Behind the Pines Assisted Living Facility, how may I help you?" a sweet-sounding voice asked, who answered on the second ring.

Kari had to suddenly clear her dry throat. "Hi, I was wondering what your hours were."

"Oh, we're always open here. There's rarely a time that you will find the front desk unmanned, so to speak. Though, it is best to come during the day if you would like to speak to someone about making arrangements for an extended stay."

Kari realized that her question was a little vague. She'd been nervous to make the call, and it was obvious. "I meant the visiting hours. What are your visiting hours for the residents?"

"I see, dear. Well, that depends largely on the person you're coming to visit. Are you coming to see family? Are they expecting you?"

"Uh, no, not exactly." Kari paused while she tried to think of what to say.

She was a little hesitant to give out too much information. She didn't want to be told that they couldn't see Lila's aunt, but she didn't want the call to sound suspicious either.

The woman on the phone mistook her hesitation for not wanting to answer.

"That's quite alright, dear. You don't have to go into the nature of your visit. We take the privacy of our residents very seriously. I was only asking to see if I could give you a little more insight into the hours that specific person kept. We have many guests who keep a varied schedule, from the early morning risers right up to the night owls. Honestly, we're oftentimes just happy to see people coming to visit at all. Many of our guests don't have a lot of visitors."

"So, we can just come whenever?"

"This isn't a prison, dear. The residents are allowed to have visitors as long as it's a decent hour. Though, it's best if you could come either before or after meals. Dinner today will be from 4 p.m. to 5 p.m. or from 6 p.m. to 7 p.m., but most of our residents tend to eat on the earlier side."

"And, if your intended visitee," the woman chuckled with her little joke, "has anything that they regularly do, we try not to upset their schedule too much. But, again, they're usually happy to receive visitors, and many welcome the distraction."

Kari breathed a sigh of relief after she realized that she didn't have to give any more details. She thanked the woman for her help.

"I just got off the phone with Behind the Pines," she told Kasi when she returned to the back room. "The woman seemed nice. She said we could go whenever, as long as we're not interfering with their routine."

"Could we close at five and head up there after?"

Kari smiled at her sister. "That's exactly what I was thinking."

At exactly five o'clock, the girls looked around. The tables were all wiped clean, all the equipment gleamed, and everything was set to open early the next morning. They locked the doors and got into Kari's Jeep to drive up to Behind the Pines.

Kari looked over at her sister, who was biting her bottom lip.

She seemed worried as she finally said, "You know she's not going to have any idea who we are, right? She might not even see us."

"Yeah, I've been thinking about that. I figured we would go and introduce ourselves and tell her that we were friends of Lila's, and we want to offer our condolences. If she seems talkative, we could ask if she knows of anyone who was upset with her niece or would wish her harm."

Kasi laughed to herself. "So, we shouldn't just jump right in and announce that we were the ones who found the body?"

Kari shot her sister a look. She had a dark sense of humor at times. It was one of her coping mechanisms, and Kari understood.

After a moment, a thought occurred to Kari. "You know, we are taking a bit of a risk going to see her."

"Yeah, I know. What if whoever went after Lila wanted to take a shot at her aunt, too? What if they were watching the facility?"

Kari switched on her blinker and turned the Jeep off the main road, following the GPS on her phone. "Well, we're not going to learn anything by not talking to her."

After a full minute of driving down the small road, Kari started to think that she had made a wrong turn or that the GPS was just wrong. Then, out of the pine groves, hidden completely from the road, sprang forth the sprawling facility.

Kasi let out a whistle. "This place is huge!"

Kari nodded in agreement. She drove the Jeep up to the small parking area near the front entrance. They both got out, looking around in amazement at the size of the place.

Just inside the front door, there was an information desk where they signed in and asked if they could see Clementine Fisher. One of the aides told them they could probably find her in the common room.

"Clementine Fisher?" Kari asked one of the employees when they walked into a large, bright room full of televisions, comfortable couches, and shelves full of books and games.

"Oh, right there," the employee said, pointing to a corner where a gray-haired woman was sitting quietly by herself.

The girls weren't sure how she would react to them being there, so they approached her cautiously.

Kari was the first to reach her. She put on her award-winning smile and said, "Hello there. I was wondering if you were Clementine Fisher, Lila Baldwin's aunt?"

The sharp-eyed woman studied Kari for a moment. There was an odd expression on her face when she answered, "That depends on who wants to know."

"My name is Kari Sweet. My sister, Kasi, and I were friends of Lila's. We wanted to offer our condolences."

"And ask a few questions," Kasi interjected, and Kari glared at her—so much for being subtle.

Clementine stared hard at the two of them before heaving a resigned sigh and responding, "That's me. So, how much do you want?"

Kari turned to her sister, who looked just as confused as she felt, then faced the woman again.

"I'm sorry, Ms. Fisher. I think you misunderstood. We were friends of your niece. We were the ones who found her, in her boutique."

Kasi interrupted, "What did you mean by how much do we want?"

Clementine chuckled at the two of them. "You two don't really seem to understand how a shakedown works. Listen, this is not my first rodeo. Heck, this isn't even my first one since my niece passed. I don't have endless amounts of time left on this earth, and I don't want to waste it.," she said blankly, shifting her gaze from Kasi to Kari. "So why don't you figure out a number quickly, so I can pay you and the other two off. But that's it! The secret stays secret after that! I'm an old woman, not some ATM. You hear me?"

"Whoa!" Kasi exclaimed.

"Ms. Fisher, my sister and I are…were friends of your niece. We aren't here to ask for money."

"Yeah, that's what the last ones said, too."

Chapter 18

Hunter

What are we missing?

Hunter was in the conference room alone, staring at the murder board that he had constructed. Though everybody at the Mills Township Police Department was officially working on the Lila Baldwin murder case, Hunter had taken something of a lead role. He had also been the one to turn the whiteboard into the aptly named 'murder board,' dedicated to collecting facts on the Baldwin case.

As information came in, Hunter updated it. However, most of what had been added up to this point was discouraging. It was primarily a board telling all the cops how little progress they had made on the case.

There has to be something… People don't get killed for no reason.

They had a timeline of events, but it mostly just had LILA MURDERED at the far-right end of the line and not much else. There was a place to list suspects, but there were no names placed on the said list yet. It reminded Hunter of a failure board, more than anything else, and he hated it.

The tox screen from the autopsy had come in earlier that day, and Hunter was holding it in his hands, reading it over for the third time.

"Nothing," he muttered to himself. "No poison, no drugs…nothing but vitamins and natural supplements… A totally clean body, at least on the inside."

This was not unexpected. Hunter would have been surprised if anything sordid had been found in Lila's body. As far as he knew, she was an upstanding citizen, with a successful local business, who showed no signs of drug use.

Still, a tox screen had to be done just to be sure. You could never assume that somebody wasn't an addict, and people could hide that sort of thing very well. However, this longshot had proven to be officially a dead end.

There seemed to be a long string of them in this case, and the autopsy had not shown anything other than what time, roughly, Lila was killed. It had been confirmed she died from a stab wound in the stomach, but Hunter could tell that just from the crime scene. They had found fingerprints, but none of them were helpful.

"No hints, no clues, no leads—at least leads that are worth anything," Hunter remarked to nobody.

Since the police had started investigating Lila Baldwin's death, they had gotten many leads. Unfortunately, they were largely, if not entirely, fruitless. Murder was an incredibly rare occurrence in Mills Township.

For most people in town, this was the first murder of their lives, and certainly, the first where the killer was a mystery. It had driven the town into a frenzy, but it had also brought a lot of unwanted attention.

It seemed like every person who wanted to make a name for themselves or get a little publicity was talking about the case. The police were being inundated with calls from people offering evidence. This included five separate calls from people claiming to know who the killer was.

Doing their due diligence, Hunter and his fellow officers had followed up on all the leads, but none of them had gone anywhere.

There was that one woman who claimed the murderer was Lila's cousin, Hunter recalled not so fondly.

The caller accused this cousin of slandering the family name. The investigation couldn't prove that Lila had a cousin, and she certainly didn't have one in town.

And let's not forget the bad leads, Hunter remembered, like the guy who claimed the killer was Jimmy Hoffa.

This was problematic for a few reasons.

For starters, Hunter wasn't sure why the former leader of the Teamsters union would want to kill Lila Baldwin. Also, Hoffa had been missing for decades, and there were a ton of rumors about his own death. Some even said that he was buried under the New York Giants' old stadium, although that had been disproven on MythBusters.

There were also some people who claimed Hoffa was still alive, making him something of a mob-tied Elvis or Andy Kaufman. This was a lead Hunter didn't bother to follow up on. It was given by someone who was clearly just a crackpot with a kooky idea.

Come on, Lila. You're gonna have to help me out here, give me something to help with this case. With leads like these, it's gonna take some divine intervention to figure out who killed you.

Sadly, the state of affairs on the hunt for Lila Baldwin's killer was looking pretty grim.

Hunter was desperate for a lead that was actually promising. He wanted to be able to put a real suspect on the murder board. They just hadn't been able to find anybody with a motive for doing it, and nobody had seen the killer.

Kari and Kasi had claimed to see a shadow moving in Lila's boutique, but you can't identify somebody by their shadow.

"Maybe they didn't even see anybody. Maybe they were just being paranoid. Your eyes can play tricks on you," Hunter mused aloud.

He stared at the board and sighed, trying to figure out what to do next.

Maybe there was some clue at the store we're overlooking. I just wish I knew what it could be.

Hunter had no experience working murder cases and trying to solve such intricate mysteries. Police work in Mills Township tended to be cut and dry. Not this time, though, and the stakes had never been higher.

If Hunter failed to find the murderer, it would be a stain on his reputation and the reputation of the entire police department. He tried to put that out of his mind. Stress just made the work harder.

"I should just call it a night," he lamented.

There was no point to him standing there, staring at his failure board.

Maybe a good night's sleep and an early morning run will help clear my mind, he pondered.

If he started fresh, he might finally get the ball rolling. However, before he could even leave the conference room, his cell phone started ringing. Pulling it out of his pocket, he noticed that it was Kari calling.

"Finally, something good's happening," Hunter said with a smile.

He could really use a break to talk to somebody about anything other than the case. Seeing Kari at her coffee house always brightened his spirits, and he was hoping to maybe get a chance to see her outside of that context again.

"Hey! I was actually just about to call you to see if you wanted to meet me at Sally's for a burger or something," Hunter cheerfully remarked.

It wasn't true that he was just about to call her, but he figured it would sound better than, "Hey, would you like to grab a bite, so I can get my mind off Lila's murder?"

Plus, he did really like the idea of having a burger with her right now. He was hungry and looking for some good company.

"Thanks for the offer, but I can't right now," Kari refused.

Hunter was surprised when he heard this. He was sure that the answer was going to be yes. He wondered why Kari couldn't meet him for a burger.

"Listen, Kasi and I are at Behind the Pines Assisted Living Facility with Clementine Fisher, Lila's aunt. You need to come here and talk to her right away," Kari said vehemently.

Hunter took a second to collect himself. His mind had been set on getting a burger with Kari, and now he was being instructed to go talk to Lila's aunt. Kari sounded almost frantic, and his senses went on high alert.

"I'm a little confused. Why do you think I need to come speak to Lila's aunt?" Hunter questioned. "What are you and Kasi doing over there anyway?"

"We came here to talk to Clementine about Lila. You know, to offer condolences. And okay, also maybe to see if there was anybody that might have had it out for Lila," Kari explained.

"Playing a bit of detective, huh?"

"No, not really. It just sort of happened that way," Kari clarified, her voice increasing in tempo. "We're afraid to leave Clementine alone right now. She just told us something crazy that you need to hear."

"What is it? Can't you just tell me?" Hunter's voice sounded worried.

"Sorry, Hunter. It's too much to talk about over the phone. You just need to get over here as soon as you can. Trust me," Kari assured.

"Okay, I'll leave right now."

Though Hunter was still a little confused, he certainly trusted Kari more than the guy who said Jimmy Hoffa had killed Lila Baldwin. He hung up the phone and grabbed his coat before heading out to his truck.

Quickly deciding to make sure he was off the clock, Hunter made a slight detour before heading out.

"This could be another dead end," he told himself.

Despite that, Hunter still wanted to follow Kari's instructions. She sounded nervous, and he wasn't going to let her down. However, he considered this a visit as a friend of the Sweet sisters rather than as a cop.

If it turned out to be a good lead, he would bring it into work, but right now, he wanted to be careful. Things had been rough enough for the department. He didn't want to add to the stress if he didn't have to.

"Hopefully, this will be the lead I've been looking for."

Chapter 19

Kari

Kari hung up her phone, having finished her conversation with Hunter. She turned back toward her sister and Clementine Fisher, who were both looking at her expectedly.

"Hunter is on his way. Don't worry, Clementine," Kari assured the older woman. "We know Hunter really well. He's a good guy and a good cop. He'll be able to help."

"I sure hope so. I don't want to be talking to any cop if they can't help me," the woman said.

Though her tone was pessimistic, Kari could understand. Here was somebody living in an assisted care facility, dealing with her beloved niece's death, yet people had apparently been coming to visit her to blackmail her for money. Now, two strange women had shown up and were inviting a police officer who was a total stranger as well.

Kari understood the skepticism Clementine had. She just hoped the woman would come to trust them.

"Clementine, would you be more comfortable waiting for Hunter back in your room?" Kasi asked patiently.

"Yes. Let's get out of here," Clementine replied, a little irritated.

The girls helped Clementine to gather her things, then they headed to her suite.

Since Kari and Kasi didn't know their way around the facility, they had to follow their new friend's lead. As they walked along, they couldn't help but noticing the splendor of Behind the Pines.

Very few details had been overlooked by the interior decorating team that had obviously put the finishing touches on the facility. There were potted plants and lush furnishings everywhere they looked. Even the carpeting was of the highest quality and was thick enough to muffle out the sound of feet as they passed by.

Wow! This place looks more like a five-star hotel that you would find in Chicago or New York City rather than an assisted living facility, Kari thought as they traversed the many hallways that led to Clementine's suite.

Finally, they stopped in front of a large double door that was apparently the entrance to Clementine's room.

Fishing out her key, Kari noticed that Clementine's hands were slightly shaking. "Is everything okay, Ms. Clementine?"

"I'm fine!" she grumbled. "I'm not an old woman that needs to be waited on hand and foot."

"I'm sorry. I didn't mean to imply anything of the sort. I just noticed that your hand was shaking. I hope we didn't upset you by coming here tonight," Kari said, apologetic.

"It's not you that I'm upset with. I'm just mad that I wasn't with Lila the night she was murdered. Instead of those crooks dealing with me, they chose to hurt my niece."

Clementine sighed, her face full of frustration and sadness, and continued, "Who'd have thought that all of the hard work we did years ago to make my golden years easier was going to come back to hurt our family? If we had known then what we know now, I'd have given it all to charity long ago. No amount of money is worth losing a loved one over."

Kari reached over and gave Clementine a comforting hug. "It's not your fault. If those swindlers are responsible for Lila's death, we'll prove it somehow, I promise. No one deserves to die like that."

Kasi quickly threw her arms around them and squeezed as tight as she could. "Lila was a good friend to us, and we're not going to stop until the murderers are caught."

After a few seconds, Clementine pulled away from the sisters and quickly opened the door.

Finally, Kari and Kasi had their first look at the room. Kari was taken aback for a moment.

It was an understatement to call it a room. Clementine basically had an apartment to herself.

Kasi followed along behind their host as Kari walked ahead and looked around a bit. They entered the living room area, which had a nice sofa and a rocking chair. The floors were covered in what appeared to be the same thick carpeting that graced the hallways, and there was a good-sized television right across from the sofa.

The living room had three large windows letting a ton of light in. On a sunny day, you wouldn't need to switch on a single light bulb.

Kari poked her head into the bedroom, which was well-decorated and featured a full-size bed, more than enough for a woman Clementine's size. The bed was festooned with pillows and a big pink comforter and a table proudly displaying pictures of Clementine's family sat next to the bed.

The room featured an en suite bathroom as well, but Kari didn't check it out. She would have had to walk through the bedroom in order to do that, and that seemed like a bit of an overreach.

Surprisingly, the suite featured a little kitchenette with a two-burner stove that seemed pristine. Kari figured it wasn't being used much, if at all.

There was a microwave, refrigerator, and freezer if Clementine needed them. It was more than enough for one person, especially since the facility offered food.

Clementine was basically living in a nice one-bedroom apartment.

Kari felt like she could see herself living in a place like this and being completely happy with it. Not that she wanted to move out from the house she shared with her sister. Living with Kasi was still the perfect thing for her at the moment.

Kasi helped Clementine to the sofa, where Lila's aunt sat down gingerly.

Hoping to make Clementine feel more at ease, Kari decided to break the ice with conversation not related to Lila's death. "Clementine, this suite is lovely."

Kasi nodded and added, "Yeah, it's super cute. I really like it."

"It should be nice, given what I have to pay for it per month." No one in the room could deny the hint of contempt in Clementine's voice.

"Oh, is this place expensive?" Kari asked.

Clementine rolled her eyes. "Is it ever? It costs you a pretty penny to get a suite like this!"

"We had no idea. I guess it would be hard for somebody on a limited budget to afford a place like this, huh?" Kari commented.

"In this tier, sure. However, there are a couple of other tiers here that aren't as pricey."

"Tier?" Kasi clarified.

"Yep. Tier Three is the least expensive one," Clementine began. "That one is pretty cheap and is for older folks who don't have a lot of money left. You get what you pay for, though. The Tier Three wing is basically like a hospital. The whole area is so drab. I try to never go over there. The rooms are cramped, and they only have a bed and a little bathroom. You have to go to the cafeteria to get your meals, and it's not even a good cafeteria."

"Yikes. That sounds rough," Kari noted.

"Tier Two isn't too bad. You have a studio apartment, basically. The rooms are a bit bigger than those of Tier Three, and you get a sofa. You also get a slightly larger bathroom. You still have your meals provided, but you get better options than Tier Three. It's not terrible, but I wouldn't want to spend the rest of my life there. Fortunately, I'm Tier One, and that's the moneymaker."

"The moneymaker?" Kari asked.

"Not for me, of course—for Behind the Pines. Those who can afford Tier One either still had a good income or planned very well for the future. Not many people can afford Tier One," Clementine said matter-of-factly.

She paused, then continued, "Fortunately, my husband had invested very well for many years. When he passed, he left most of his money to me, since we didn't have children. It allowed me my choice of where I would live for the rest of my life. After Ben, that was my husband, passed, Behind the Pines suddenly showed up to make their pitch."

Curious, Kasi asked, "Behind the Pines came to you?"

"Yeah, they offered to give me a tour of the facility," Clementine answered. "They must be keeping an eye on the obituaries or something. They're kind of vultures, to be honest."

Kari was somewhat surprised that some facilities actually did that, but she didn't interrupt Clementine and let her finish.

"When I visited, they only showed me Tier One, and, of course, they made it look so nice. Looking back, I guess they must have known that I had money. Anyway, my old house was so big it didn't make sense for me to live there all alone, so I decided to sell it. Then, I moved in here."

"At least you were able to afford Tier One, and you seem to be happy with your living situation," Kari suggested.

"I guess. Had I known about the tier system, I might not have moved here. I thought the whole facility was like this, big suites and happy residents. Then I moved in and realized I had been mistaken. A lot of the people in the lower tiers resent us in Tier One. I can't say I blame them. They're stuck here, and every day, they're reminded about how much better others have it."

The sisters looked at each other. It was obvious that both Kari and Kasi were feeling pretty bad for Clementine. Even if she had a nice place to live in, it was hard for her to enjoy it considering the circumstances.

"When is your friend, the cop, going to get here?" Clementine asked.

"It should be soon. We just need to wait a little longer," Kari replied.

"Well, I certainly hope so."

Clementine seemed tired of having guests. As they waited for Hunter to arrive, Kari couldn't help thinking of Lila's murder. Maybe money was the reason Lila was killed.

If she was Clementine's only heir, was it possible that was the motive for Lila's murder?

What if someone went to Lila's boutique to blackmail her as well? Maybe that person threatened to hurt Clementine if Lila didn't get them some cash.

Someone was already blackmailing Clementine. Could Lila have found out about that and known who had done it? And could they have killed Lila when she confronted them?

Kari's mind was racing. She hoped that Hunter would be able to make sense of it all when he got there.

Chapter 20

Kari

When is Hunter going to get here? I hope nothing bad has happened, Kari thought to herself.

She and her sister were still sitting with Clementine, waiting for Hunter to arrive. Apparently, Clementine was being blackmailed to keep a family secret. Could this have something to do with Lila's murder?

Unfortunately, it was taking Hunter longer to get to Behind the Pines Assisted Living Facility than anticipated, so the Sweets were left to metaphorically twiddle their thumbs in the meantime.

Suddenly, Kari remembered something. "Hey, Agnes Gaines lives here, right?" she asked Kasi.

Agnes was a lovely woman that Kari and Kasi rented their house from. Much like Clementine, she had decided to downsize once a whole house became too much for her to handle, and so Agnes had moved to Behind the Pines. At least that was how Kari recalled things; she just needed to check it with Kasi to be sure.

"Yeah, I'm almost positive this is the place," Kasi confirmed.

"We should go and say hi to her," Kari suggested. "It's been a while since we've seen Agnes. Plus, now that I know about the tiers, I'm worried about her. I hope she's in Tier One."

Kasi agreed. "Me too. She's such a nice woman. It'd be awful if she was, like, stuck in Tier Three or something."

With that, she hopped up from the couch.

"I'll go look for Agnes' room and check in on her."

Kari was going to respond, wondering why they couldn't both go see Agnes.

However, before she could get a word out, Kasi bent down and whispered in her ear, "I don't think we should leave Clementine alone. We don't know who we can trust in this place, and we already know that she's been approached for money. I'll go see Agnes. You should stay here to make sure Clementine is safe."

Kari nodded in agreement. She was glad that Kasi was on the ball.

The sisters were a good team. Both were bright and determined women, but by working together, they were always able to cover for occasional lapses in insight.

Kasi left Clementine's suite, leaving Kari to talk with the woman they had just met.

"Kasi's going to go see our landlady, Agnes. I'm going to stay here and keep you company," Kari informed.

"That's awful nice of you," Clementine replied.

Since the two ladies didn't have a ton in common, the only thing that Kari could think of to talk to Clementine about was her niece. It was the one topic of discussion that would be easy for the them both— well, relatively easy. The fact that Lila had been murdered would hang over the conversation, but there was still so much good to talk about when it came to the late Miss Baldwin.

"I loved Lila's shop," Kari began. "The Style Factory was so cool. My sister and I considered it one of our favorite stores in Mills Township. Heck, it was one of our favorite stores we've ever been to."

"That's good to hear," Clementine acknowledged. "I was only able to make it to the store a couple of times a week. Whenever I was there, I was always the oldest person around—not that I felt out of place. I always like being around young people. Keeps me on my toes."

"Lila was always so nice to us when we were there, too. She treated us like her favorite customers. Sometimes, when I saw an item I liked but I couldn't buy it right away, she would hold it for me until I could come by and pick them up. It was so sweet of her," Kari added.

Clementine nodded. "She was a great and caring person. I saw her like a daughter, and sometimes I felt like she saw me as a second mother or, at least, like her favorite aunt. She always treated me so well. In fact, she used to visit me every day."

Hearing this made Kari feel good. Even though Clementine had one of the nicest suites in the facility, it would still be awful for her to never get any visitors. Knowing that Lila always made time for her aunt gave Kari a warm feeling inside. It was too bad she was gone, though. At least she'd made her Aunt's life brighter while she was alive. Kari realized that was all anybody could really do.

Lila really was a great person. The more Kari thought of it, the less it made sense anybody could even think of killing her.

"In fact, a lot of times, Lila would come over, and then she would take me out to Sally's Diner for burgers, even though she knew my doctor didn't want me to have them. Of course, if it was up to my doctor, I would never eat food with any taste to it again. Doctors seem to think that if it tastes good, I shouldn't be eating it," Clementine joked.

Kari let out a little chuckle. She hoped that she had as much spirit in her when she was Clementine's age. The two continued chatting about Lila when, suddenly, Kasi reappeared at the door.

"Did you find Agnes?" Kari asked her sister.

"Yeah, I did. I could only spend a few minutes with her, but it was nice to see her. I told her you said hello, of course."

"I hope you explained why I wasn't able to be there with you. I would hate for Agnes to think I didn't want to see her," Kari countered.

"No, I told her the truth. I told her that you won the lottery, and now you were a big shot that didn't have time for anybody else," Kasi replied with a smile.

Kari rolled her eyes and laughed at her sister's quick wit. "Ha, ha. Very funny."

"Of course, I told her why you weren't able to see her." Kasi turned to face Clementine. "Agnes told me to tell you hello, by the way, Clementine."

"Ah, good ol' Agnes. We play bridge together quite often," Clementine shared. "Actually, she's probably my favorite bridge partner. We work well together. We always seem to run the table."

"You two are the Harlem Globetrotters of the local bridge scene, huh? I bet everybody else is afraid to play you guys," Kari remarked.

"Oh, there are no hard feelings. I don't think anybody has ever gotten mad when we beat them," Clementine noted eagerly. "We just play for fun—or sometimes pretzel sticks—and honestly, a good game of bridge can be as much excitement as some people get around here."

The talk of bridge seemed to uplift Clementine's spirits, and this made Kari and Kasi happy and relieved.

"Unfortunately," Clementine continued, "a lot of folks in this facility have no family left, or if they have family, they never come to visit. They're alone most of the time. A good game of bridge is a highlight of their week, even if Agnes and I dominate them."

"Aw, that's so sad. I can't imagine anybody not wanting to come visit their parents," Kari said apologetically.

"Yeah. I mean, Kari and I just went to see our parents yesterday. These poor, lonely people. Now I want to visit them all!" Kasi added.

"Well, it's not that their families are all ungrateful. Many of them just saw their families move away," Clementine noted.

155

Kasi chimed in, "That's what Agnes told me. She said that she doesn't get a lot of guests since her kids moved far away. I think one moved to Charlotte and another moved to Denver."

"We should come visit her more often then. Let's make sure to do that, sis," Kari proposed.

"Absolutely. By the way, Agnes is in Tier Two. Her room doesn't have a homey feeling to it at all. It's super drab," Kasi remarked, adding a gagging motion to fully express her distaste for Tier Two.

"Ugh, that's terrible. At least it isn't Tier Three, though," Kari said.

"I think we should go buy her some stuff to make her room seem more like a real home," Kasi recommended. "Like we could get a couple of rugs and some throw pillows for her couch. Right now, the couch is so bland. Imagine some bright red pillows on it! We should get her some new bedding, too—a nice, cozy comforter that will keep her warm all winter."

Kari realized her sister's mind was going a mile a minute with ideas. If she didn't step in, Kasi would spend a thousand dollars mentally. She couldn't help herself.

"That sounds great. Let's do that as soon as we can," Kari agreed.

"Wow, aren't you two girls just the sweetest? I'd love to have somebody like you in my family," Clementine told the sisters.

Sadly, this brought Kari again to the realization that Clementine Fisher's family just got a little smaller. Kari made a mental note to also visit her more often and maybe even take her to Sally's Diner.

The two sisters smiled at Clementine's compliment. They genuinely wanted to do something nice for Agnes, so it wasn't about getting accolades. Still, it was nice to know that their hypothetical efforts were being rewarded.

Kari figured somebody had to step up for these folks. Why shouldn't it be her and Kasi?

Chapter 21

Kari

Kari looked down at her watch for the umpteenth time. It seemed like forever since she had called, and Hunter still hadn't shown up. She was getting antsy and worried.

What's taking him so long?

Kari could only hope everything was okay.

Hunter's a cop. she told herself. *Maybe he had something to do before coming here.*

The Sweet sisters continued their small talk with Clementine about her niece Lila.

"Clementine, tell us about Lila when she was a little girl. Did she ever get into trouble?"

"Oh, did she ever? That girl had a heart of gold but a temper like a rattlesnake. She used to love playing outside and climbing trees."

"Wow! Who would have ever thought that the stylish woman we knew from the shop was a tomboy as a kid?"

"I know, but that was my Lila. She loved getting dirty and playing outside. I think it gave her an appreciation for things that kids these days just don't have."

"Kari and I were just saying something like this the other day, Clementine. Some of these kids today just don't appreciate anything."

"I agree, ladies. Sadly, I think that is a thing of the past with this new generation." Clementine said. "But at least most of them don't have to go without or worry about going to bed hungry. That makes it worth it in my estimation. I guess I'd rather have spoiled kids than suffering ones."

Kari and Kasi both thought that was a good observation. They hadn't really thought about it from that perspective. It gave them insight into how Lila had become such a good person.

They had only known Lila as an adult, but that was enough for them to come to really like her. She had been a great mentor and an even better friend. Kari and Kasi were really enjoying all the stories Clementine was telling.

However, Kari was beginning to worry that she and Kasi might end up wearing out their welcome with Clementine. She was a nice woman, just like her niece, but Kari was concerned that Clementine would get tired of having them around. Her gruff demeanor from earlier had vanished, but Kari guessed that would only hold for so long.

On top of that, Clementine could end up getting too down if they had to keep talking about Lila for too long. After all, Lila was Clementine's niece, and she loved her.

Now, Lila was dead—murdered, to be more specific. It must be hard for Clementine to deal with that. The sisters certainly had their issues dealing with Lila's death in its aftermath.

What if Clementine got too sad and didn't want to talk anymore? That would hurt the investigation, and Kari couldn't imagine pressing poor Clementine Fisher to talk if she didn't want to.

I should take the initiative, Kari resolved.

She was worried about these mysterious visitors that Clementine had gotten. This was why Hunter was called over in the first place. It seemed like a break in the case.

Somebody had come to ask Clementine for money and threatened to reveal a family secret if she didn't. If it was a family secret, Lila surely knew it.

What if the people who had extorted Clementine moved on to Lila? Kari contemplated. They might've been more willing to get violent with somebody who wasn't elderly.

At the moment, she was primarily concerned that the people who tried to get money out of Clementine might come back and that they might be even bolder this time. They might even do the sweet woman harm. Kari couldn't let that happen.

She decided that she should ask Clementine about these visitors herself. That way, in a worse-case scenario, she could relay information to Hunter. She wanted to know what had happened, even if she was aware that she was getting too close to playing detective.

"Clementine, I hesitate to bring this up, but do you remember anything about the people who came by to get money from you? For example, do you remember what they looked like?" Kari asked.

"Yeah, I remember exactly what they looked like," Clementine replied.

Kari and Kasi looked at each other, surprised.

"Why do you look so shocked?" Clementine inquired. "Just because I'm old doesn't mean I'm losing my memory."

161

Kari and Kasi now had their looks changed from shocked to uncomfortable. Fortunately, Clementine let out a laugh.

"I'm just joking with you girls," she said with a smile.

Kari felt relieved. The last thing she wanted to do was make Clementine think that she thought less of the older woman because of her age.

"There were two of them: a man and a woman," Clementine recalled. "They were probably about your age, maybe a little older."

Kari and Kasi were both in their twenties, but they were also five years apart in age. So, Clementine saying these mysterious people were about their age, maybe a little older, was a little unclear. Kari didn't want to derail Clementine's train of thought, so she just kept quiet and let her continue talking.

"The man was on the shorter side, and the woman was about the same height. I can't tell you any specific numbers. I would probably be way off. I've been shrinking for a few years, so now everybody seems taller to me than they used to. The guy was also on the heavier side a little bit. Not fat but not thin."

Kari, trying to help Clementine out, suggested, "Paunchy?"

"Yes, that's the right word—paunchy. Fun word, too," she said with a laugh.

"The woman was skinny, though, and had long brown hair. I don't remember what color her eyes were. It seems my memory isn't the best after all. The man was wearing a ball cap and sunglasses. I should have realized something was fishy then."

Kari realized she should be taking these details down. She got her phone out and used the notes app to write down the description of the two people who had visited Clementine.

"Have you ever seen them before? Were they people you knew?" Kasi asked, joining the conversation.

"No, I don't believe I've ever seen them before that first visit. They seemed new to me. However, they ended up making three visits overall," Clementine recollected.

"I remember the first one clearly. I was told I had guests, which I wasn't expecting, but I didn't mind. Besides, when they showed up, they were very friendly. They told me they were friends of Lila, and that they just wanted to come visit her favorite aunt. Now, that did seem odd to me, since I'm Lila's only aunt. But heck, I thought they were just trying to be clever. You know, making a joke about my being her favorite aunt because I'm her only aunt."

"And then what happened?" Kari followed up.

"Well, the first visit was fine, so when they came for a second visit, I was surprised, but I didn't mind. They were nice people. At least, that was what I thought. They were much less friendly on this second visit."

Kari watched as Clementine's demeanor changed.

"They both kept asking me questions about my family. For some reason, they had a ton of questions, and they kept asking if I had other guests besides Lila. I wanted to be polite, because that's my nature, so I told them that I was lucky to have more visitors than most at this facility. That wasn't enough for them, though. They kept pressing me for specifics. They were obsessed with my guests. So finally, I told them I was tired and that they had to leave."

Kari looked at her sister, who had instinctively looked over at her as well. They both wore a worried expression. This sounded bad already, and Clementine hadn't even gotten to the point where they asked her for money yet.

"So, what happened with the final visit?" Kari asked.

"This time, they didn't even bother pretending to be nice. They came, and right away, the guy started talking to me so angrily. He said that they knew my secret, and then if I didn't pay them off, I would regret it. I tried to reason with them, but they

164

wouldn't have it. I'm in no position to fight back at my age. There was really nothing I could do," Clementine explained.

What the girls wanted to know was why Clementine was so determined to keep this secret. To understand that, they would have to know what the secret was.

However, they couldn't just come right out and ask. That would have been rude. Still, the question was hanging in the air.

"Miss Clementine, what secret are they talking about?" Kasi finally, timidly, asked.

Thank goodness, she has more guts than me! Kari thought.

Fortunately for Kari, Kasi was slightly less worried about appearing rude.

Of course, the ball was still in Clementine's court. She could keep the secret if she wanted. The girls weren't going to press her or extort her.

We're better than those creeps, Kari thought.

Clementine was about to answer. Kari had a mix of anticipation and fear inside her. Then, before she could say a word, there was a knock on the door.

A jolt ran up Kari's spine. She had been so engaged in the conversation that she had been startled by the knock.

165

Who's at the door? Is it Hunter? That would be great!

On the other hand, with all the talk of shakedowns and murder, it was hard for Kari not to be afraid. As she slowly rose from her seat, a sense of dread filled her gut.

Chapter 22

Hunter

"I hope I'm not too late," Hunter muttered to himself as he arrived at Clementine Fisher's door.

He had made it over as soon as he could break away from things at the office. Kari and Kasi told him that he needed to come talk to Clementine, and though Hunter had been left in the dark a bit, he knew it was related to the murder of Lila Baldwin. That was good enough for him as long as there was an actual lead to be found in this conversation.

The investigation into Lila's murder had been immensely frustrating for Hunter. The murder board down at the police department was lacking suspects. Any calls providing leads had proven false.

Hunter felt better about this one. He trusted the Sweet sisters. They didn't feel like the kind of people who would lie or embellish stories.

Still, Hunter was doing this off the books since he didn't want to be on the clock if this was another bad lead.

Here goes nothing. He thought.

Hunter knocked and waited. He heard some murmuring inside, but it was taking a while for somebody to answer the door. Finally, he heard some footsteps, which sounded tentative, approaching the door.

"Hello?" a voice called out.

He could tell it was Kari's. Hunter would recognize her voice anywhere.

"Hey, Kari. It's Hunter."

"Oh, Hunter!"

The door flung open, and Hunter saw Kari greeting him with a smile. Hunter returned her smile as he stepped into the suite.

He looked around. It seemed nice and not what he had expected in an assisted living facility.

Hunter peered into the living room, where he saw Kasi sitting in a beautiful wingback chair. Across from her on the sofa was an older woman. Hunter quickly deduced it was Clementine, the woman he was here to meet.

"Sorry, I ran a little late. I had to handle some work stuff before I came over," Hunter explained. "The big boss cornered me for a chat on the way out, but I'm here now."

"That's okay. There's still time to talk," Kari remarked. "You've got to hear what she has to say."

Hunter made his way over to Clementine and extended his hand. She didn't make a move to get up, which was understandable. She had lived long enough to dictate what she did and when she did it, and this was a right she had earned.

"Hi. I'm Hunter Houston. I'm a police officer in Mills Township and a friend of Kari and Kasi."

Clementine looked Hunter dead in the eyes with determination and grabbed his hand to shake it. For a woman her age, she had an incredibly strong handshake.

"Clementine Fisher. Glad to make your acquaintance," she said.

Though Hunter had just met Clementine, he already liked her. There was something about the way she carried herself that Hunter admired.

Clementine had a lot of fire left in her, and if her body allowed, Hunter imagined Clementine would be a real handful for anybody to deal with. He hoped to be half as fiery and sharp at her age.

"Alright, Ms. Fisher, the reason I'm here is because Kari and Kasi thought I should come talk to you.

They think it might help me find who killed your niece Lila Baldwin. Is that true?"

Hunter was looking at Clementine when he spoke, but it was Kari who jumped in to answer his question.

"We talked to Clementine about this while we were waiting for you to get here. She told us everything!"

"Yeah! Two people came to visit her: a man and a woman. The man was short and paunchy and wore a hat and glasses. The woman had long brown hair and was skinny," Kasi added.

"They told Clementine that they were friends of Lila's and that they wanted to visit her favorite aunt," Kari noted. "They were all friendly and stuff at first, but then things got weird after that."

"The second time they came, they were asking her a bunch of questions about her family and who came to visit her," Kasi said. "They were aggressive and were asking for a ton of details. Clementine didn't know what they wanted, so she asked them to leave."

Kari chimed in, "So they came back a third time and threatened her. The man and the woman said that if Clementine didn't give them money, they would reveal her secret and that she'd regret it. They threatened her for cash. Clementine thought we came to extort money from her when we met her. That's why this all came out."

While Kari and Kasi were excitedly recounting the details of their conversation, Hunter had sat down on the couch near Clementine. He quietly listened to everything they had to say.

Hunter looked over at Clementine while the sisters were talking. She seemed to have an amused look on her face. Hunter couldn't help being entertained by the enthusiasm of the Sweet girls as well.

"Are they always like this?" Clementine asked.

"Yes, ma'am, I imagine they are. I've just never seen them quite this excited before."

"Well, I believe they got all the facts straight anyway. I don't believe I could have told it any better myself."

Hunter was thinking this seemed like a good lead for once. There was no direct connection between Clementine being shaken down for cash and Lila's murder, but two members of the same family were victims of crimes. They could be connected.

Hunter was looking for any sort of help on the case, and this was the most promising thing he had heard yet. That being said, there were more questions to be answered. Hunter couldn't just hear this story and leave.

"Ms. Fisher, these people that threatened you, do you think they had more than idle words? Maybe they wouldn't have gotten rough with you, but could they have gone after Lila looking for money as well, and could they have gotten physical with her? Perhaps even murdered her?"

Hunter realized that making Clementine consider the possibility that the man and woman who threatened her had also killed her niece could be troubling. That would mean Ms. Fisher had met Lila's murderers.

On the other hand, that would mean Clementine could identify them, which would go a long way toward getting them arrested. Clementine seemed to be deep in thought for a moment. She was really mulling the question over.

"I suppose it's possible. If Lila didn't want to pay them, and if she didn't want the secret to get out, things could have gotten serious."

Hunter knew he had to broach the subject of the secret. He felt like he had to know what it was if he was going to make any progress on this case. He just had to hope Clementine was willing to share it.

Unlike a heartless criminal, he wasn't going to press her or threaten her.

"Ma'am, I hesitate to ask, but could you tell me what kind of secret would be considered so important as to blackmail someone over and to possibly even kill someone?"

Clementine took a deep breath. Hunter could tell she was uncomfortable. He hated putting somebody through this, but murder investigations were never easy on people.

Finally, Clementine began speaking.

"Decades ago—it was more than fifty-five years ago by this point—I had a baby. This was back when I was still a teenager. I wasn't married, and the father was out of the picture. There were no unwed teenage mothers back in those days."

Her face darkened a bit as she continued, "I could have tried to marry a man and pass the baby off as his, but I didn't want to do that. Some parents would raise their child's baby and pretend it was theirs, but that wasn't in the cards for me. I had no choice. I had to give my baby up for adoption."

Hunter and the Sweets sat quietly and listened to Clementine's story. It was already a real bombshell.

"I gave my baby up, and once I got older, I tried to find the child. However, there was no information available," Clementine explained. "When I was twenty, I married Edgar, and I told him about my secret. Together, we tried to find her, but we kept hitting dead ends. Eventually, I gave up."

"Wow. That's certainly quite the secret to keep all these years," Kari commented.

173

"Do you think that your secret child may have had anything to do with Lila's death?" Hunter asked.

"Possibly. There is one thing I can think of."

"What is it?" Hunter questioned, leaning forward.

"Well, not long before Lila was murdered, I had updated my will. Since Lila's my only living relative, I named her my new sole beneficiary," Clementine revealed.

Hunter's eyes went wide a bit. Money was often a motive for murder, and if Lila was the sole beneficiary of Clementine's will, there was certainly a lot of cash involved. Hunter knew from experience where there was money, there was motive.

Chapter 23

Kari

Kari glanced at her sister. She could tell that Clementine was exhausted from their visit and that revealing her past had taken all her energy. She was slumped in her chair and looked like she needed a nap.

"Thank you, Clementine, for sharing this with us," Hunter said, patting the woman's hand. "I promise you I will do everything in my power to find the people who threatened you and make sure they never come near you again."

Clementine looked at him with adoration, and Kari's heart sped up.

He's such a good guy, she thought.

"Thank you, officer," Clementine said, her voice shaking. "I hated keeping that secret my entire life. It hurts my heart so much to know my daughter was out there somewhere. At least now, people will know the truth."

Hunter turned to the sisters.

"Why don't you two head home?" he suggested. "I really appreciate you calling this to my attention. It's a huge break in the case. I'll see you both tomorrow when I stop by for my coffee, okay?"

Kasi beamed at her sister with pride. Kari returned the smile, though hers was tempered by uncertainty. They'd just thrown themselves in the middle of a murder investigation.

Did they have any business snooping around? What if they'd put themselves in danger?

"Do you feel like we're letting her down?" Kasi asked as they walked out of the retirement community.

"Who?" Kari asked.

As soon as they'd walked into the brisk evening air, she'd felt a wave of exhaustion hit her. She wanted nothing more than to get home, put on her most comfortable sweats, and drink a cup of hot tea.

"Clementine, of course. I mean, we left her there all alone."

"She's not all alone," Kari corrected. "She's with a whole community of people. Besides, Hunter said he was going to send a patrol on a regular basis just in case. We didn't want to leave her alone, but it's not like we could move into her room."

"I know, but I feel like there's something more we should be doing." Kasi pulled on her bottom lip, a nervous habit she'd had since she was a little girl.

"There's nothing more we can do tonight," Kari assured her. "Why don't we plan on coming back tomorrow after we close? If nothing else, we can keep her company and bring over some yummy treats for Agnes."

Kasi seemed to be happy with this plan. The two of them walked briskly to the Jeep, their heads bowed against the sudden cold breeze.

"Kari, wait," Kasi suddenly hissed just as her sister was reaching for the handle on the driver's side door.

When Kasi looked up, her sister gestured to the nearby alley where two shapes were barely illuminated by the streetlights.

"What do you think they're doing there?" Kasi whispered. "It looks really suspicious."

Kari looked around, hoping to see that Hunter hadn't left yet.

When she didn't see his truck, she shrugged and said, "Only one way to find out. HEY! WHAT ARE YOU TWO DOING OVER THERE?"

At her shout, Kasi cringed. "Kari!" she cried. "What are you doing?"

"They could be here to hurt Clementine!" Kari pointed out. "Let's go find out."

Kasi reluctantly followed her sister as they approached the suspicious duo. As they got closer, the two lurkers took off at a run. Without really thinking about it, the Sweet sisters gave chase.

"What...are...we...doing?" Kasi gasped when they finally stopped at an alley behind a large building. "This is crazy!"

Kari, also struggling to catch her breath, shook her head. "I don't know! I wasn't thinking. I just acted! My adrenaline kicked in."

"Well, we acted stupidly," Kasi remarked. "I mean, look where we are!"

She gestured around to the piles of garbage and lack of streetlights in the alley and said, "This is not safe."

She was proven correct when they heard heavy footsteps behind them. The girls spun around and saw the two shady figures they'd been chasing.

"Oh my god, Kari! He has a knife!" Kasi whispered frantically.

Kari saw that her sister was right. One of the figures, clearly a man, was holding a large knife, the blade gleaming in the faint light coming from the nearby street.

As he and his companion advanced, Kari shouted, "STOP! Or else!" She knew it sounded foolish, but she was so scared that she had no control what came out of her mouth.

"Or else what?" the man sneered. "Are you gonna try to call your boyfriend? He's gone. We already saw him leave, and we know the old bat told you her secret. That means we have to get rid of you, too."

Kari heard her sister start crying quietly beside her.

"I love you, Kar," she said tearfully. "You're the best sister a girl could ask for."

Kari wasn't about to give up that easily, though. She knew the best thing they could do was buy themselves some time. She'd gotten them into the mess, and she would do everything in her power to at least get her sister out of it.

"What do you have against a poor lady in a retirement home?" she asked. "She never hurt anyone!"

The two didn't answer. Instead, they closed the gap between themselves and the sisters. As they got close enough to grab their arms, Kari saw they matched the description of the couple who were harassing Clementine.

As Kari felt a knife dig into the small of her back, she knew she had to think fast.

"Yes, we know Clementine's secret," she admitted. "But what does that have to do with the two of you? She told us that she hadn't named a beneficiary before she changed her will to give Lila everything. So, it's not like Lila was getting someone else's money."

"That's where you're wrong," the woman hissed. "The money would have gone to her closest living relative. And guess who that would have been?"

Kasi gasped. "You're…you're Clementine's granddaughter?"

The woman nodded. "That old woman threw my mother away like she was trash. Then she goes and gets rich, and we never see a dime! I deserve some of that money after all the hardship we went through before my mom died!"

"We deserve it," the man corrected her. "You and me, sweetie. Once we get all that money, it's nothing but tropical sunsets and pina coladas for us!"

"But she tried to find your mother!" Kari protested. "She said she looked for her everywhere!"

"Yeah, right!" the woman said with a snort. "She mustn't have looked very hard. It's not like we were hiding or anything, unless you call living in a one-bedroom rat-infested apartment hiding!"

"Why didn't you just tell her who you were?" Kari probed. "I'm sure she would have welcomed you with open arms! She would have given you however much money you wanted!"

"You seem pretty sure about that," the woman answered. "I'm not so sure. People have treated me like dirt my whole life. What would make her any different? In this life, you have to take what you want. That's what my mom taught me. That stupid boutique owner was going to get everything. How is that fair? She had a nice shop, a nice house. She didn't need any of that! She didn't deserve it!"

Kari heard the distant rumble of a car engine. They were only about fifty feet from the nearest street, though there hadn't been a vehicle on it since they'd been in the alley. Now, though, she saw distant lights quickly approaching.

"After Clementine goes, I'll get it all. My mom would be proud!"

After Clementine goes? Kari was horrified at the thought. They were planning to kill her as well!

The sound of the car got closer, and their two attackers turned toward the headlights that appeared over the hill.

Kari took the opportunity to stomp hard on the man's foot, and he released his grip on her. Before the woman could react, Kari grabbed her sister's arm and yanked her away, dragging her down the alley at a sprint.

"HELP!" Kari cried, hearing footsteps closing in behind them. "HELP US!"

They made it to the street, just in time to see Hunter's truck skid to a halt, and his door fly open.

"They're trying to KILL US!" Kasi screamed hysterically.

Kari looked behind her to see the couple veer off in the other direction.

"Those are the killers!" she yelled at Hunter. "Don't let them get away!"

"Get back to the facility!" Hunter instructed, jumping back into Babe.

Kari and Kasi watched him take off in hot pursuit then looked at each other in astonishment. Before Kari could say a word, Kasi collapsed, sobbing into her arms.

Chapter 24
Hunter

As Hunter was driving away from Behind the Pines, a thought popped into his head. Suddenly, he felt like an idiot.

"I should've asked for security camera footage!" he yelled at himself. "I'm a fool." He said and hit the steering wheel.

Big facilities like Behind the Pines almost always have security cameras, at least in certain public areas. They very likely had one where visitors arrived, to say the least.

Granted, security footage was often deleted after a period of time, but maybe they still had some that would feature the man and the woman who had threatened Clementine and asked her for cash. At the very least, it was a huge mistake for him not to look.

It was so obvious. *Come on, man. Get your head in the game!*

Hunter decided to turn around and grab the footage right now. The two people in question likely knew there was a chance of getting caught on security footage, so they probably tried to hide their faces. Still, any footage was better than none.

Hunter was casually pulling into the parking lot when, suddenly, he was jolted by some figures moving in the shadows.

"What the heck?" he muttered aloud.

He slammed on the brakes and watched what was unfolding. Hunter noticed two people running in the direction of his car. As they got closer, Hunter could see it was Kari and Kasi, and he could see fear in their faces.

"Help us! Somebody help us!" the sisters cried.

Immediately, Hunter jumped into action. He pulled his truck between the girls and whatever they were running from. Suddenly, he saw two people heading his direction.

One of them was a man, and the other one was a woman. They were similar to the couple that Kari and Kasi had described earlier—the ones that had threatened Clementine. Of course, the fact that these two individuals were currently chasing down the girls had helped tip Hunter off.

Even if they were two different people, right now, they were in Hunter's crosshairs, metaphorically speaking.

Then, Hunter noticed a glimmer of light in the hands of the man. That was enough for Hunter to believe the man had a weapon.

He put his truck into park. Previously, he had been idling in case he needed to take off driving and jumped out.

"Freeze! Mills Township Police! Get on the ground!"

Kari and Kasi had made their way behind Hunter's truck to hide. He'd told them to go inside, but they were safe enough behind the vehicle. Running into the building would have left them too exposed anyway.

The couple stopped dead in their tracks. Up close and out of his car, Hunter could tell the man had a knife in his hand.

"Drop the knife and get on the ground! I won't ask again!"

The couple did not stop, however, but instead turned around and began booking it full speed for a car on the other side of the parking lot.

"Stop! I said stop!" Hunter yelled once more.

His orders fell on deaf ears. If they were going to run, he was going to pursue. He couldn't make it to them and stop them before they got in their car, and

Hunter knew he couldn't get backup to Behind the Pines in time.

Nobody on the force even knew he was there. Hunter realized the best thing to do was to pursue them in his own vehicle and then call in backup for a good, old-fashioned police chase. Hunter would need the help, since he was driving Babe, not his police car.

Hunter turned back toward Kari and Kasi.

"You two get back inside and stay there until I get back. You got that?"

They quickly made their way from behind the truck and toward the front door of the living facility. Now that the killers were fleeing, the sisters had a clear path to the doors. Hunter jumped back in his truck and took off.

The fleeing criminals had just started their car as well, so he wasn't too far behind. The car sped out of the parking lot, tires screeching, and Hunter began the pursuit.

Hunter was worried, because the woman behind the wheel was driving awfully fast. He needed to keep pace, which meant two cars were speeding through the streets, and neither of them were a cop car. Somebody might get hurt.

Stop signs and traffic lights weren't going to be followed. Hunter knew he had to get more law enforcement officers in on the chase immediately. That would end things as quickly and safely as possible.

Hunter jumped on his phone and explained the situation, "I'm in pursuit of the suspects in the Lila Baldwin murder case, and they have just fled from Behind the Pines Assisted Living Facility in a black 2005 Dodge Neon."

It may not seem like much of a car, but the couple really seemed to be giving it all it could handle.

The chase was pushing Hunter's truck, too, but he knew Babe could handle it until the Mills Township Police Department could get cars on the scene. A couple of minutes of chasing later, Hunter started to hear the sirens in the distance.

It's game over now! he thought triumphantly.

The sound grew louder and louder. Then, he could see the lights. There were police cruisers coming from both directions.

The man and the woman had nowhere to go. They were surrounded. The only real question left was whether they would go quietly or throw caution to the wind and let things end ugly.

Fortunately, they opted for the former. The car pulled over to the side of the road and stopped. Hunter pulled up his truck right behind them.

The couple got out of the car with their hands raised. Hunter approached them with cuffs in hand and placed them on the wrists of the man while reading him his rights. His fellow officer, Jo, approached the car to handcuff the woman.

"What's going on here, Hunter?"

"Jo, these two threatened Clementine Fisher, and I believe they're also the ones who murdered Lila Baldwin. I saw them chasing two women through a parking lot, and the man here was carrying a knife with him. Take them down to the station. I need to check on the two women who are still at Behind the Pines."

Hunter hopped back in his truck and hurried to Behind the Pines. When he arrived, he found Kari and Kasi inside with a couple of security officers, as well as Clementine and another woman whom he didn't recognize.

Kari and Kasi seemed shaken up, and they were both being hugged by the two women. Agnes, as he later found out, was talking about how brave both were.

"We caught them. Those two are going down to the station to be booked. They're definitely getting locked up for something, but we need to get your statements," Hunter told Kari and Kasi.

"I'm okay with that, but I don't think I'm ready to drive. I'm too shaken," Kari said in a trembling voice.

"Me too," Kasi added.

"No problem. If it's okay with security, we'll just leave your Jeep here, Kari, and I will drive you to the station," Hunter suggested.

"That's fine with us, sir. We'll keep an eye on the vehicle."

The two girls hopped into Hunter's truck, with Kari getting in the passenger seat. When they got to the station, Pete Michaels took Kasi to get her statement, while Kari stayed with Hunter.

Kari explained everything. She told Hunter about how she and her sister were threatened with a knife and how the woman had explained she was the daughter of Clementine's secret child. She had killed Lila so that she would be the sole beneficiary of Clementine's will and get all her money.

Hunter took the statement down dutifully. It wasn't enough to charge the two with murder, but Hunter figured if they pressed, they could secure a murder charge, especially if they were still using the same knife that they had used to kill Lila. The knife they had found after the chase was now in police evidence.

Things were looking up.

"Are you doing okay?" Hunter asked Kari, deeply worried.

"I think I'll be fine...thanks to you."

Hunter smiled, and Kari smiled back.

"I have to stay and finish some paperwork, so a patrol unit is going to take you and Kasi home," Hunter informed.

"Okay. Thanks for getting that set up for us," Kari said.

"Don't worry about it. I'll see you tomorrow," Hunter promised. "I'm glad you two are safe."

Pete and Kasi walked over to where they were sitting, having finished with her statement. It was time for Kari and Kasi to head home, but Hunter was almost reluctant to let them leave.

He knew they were in good hands, though. Hunter thanked Pete for his help and said good night to the Sweet girls.

As they walked off to leave, Hunter turned back to his desk and his paperwork. The case was almost over, but he still had a long night ahead of him.

Chapter 25

Kari

"Hey, Kasi, could you get me the vacuum cleaner? We've got a situation here," Kari called out to her sister, who was in the storage room.

Kari was busy trying to clean up a table full of glitter powder, which was left by a group of overly enthusiastic cosplayers who had come in the coffee shop earlier that afternoon. One of them accidentally ruined his costume while in the shop, spilling glitter all over the table.

"I don't know, Kari. I kinda like the shop's shiny new décor," Kasi joked as she approached the unfortunate table with a vacuum cleaner in hand.

"You know what, it does look kind of good. Let's spill glitter on the rest of the tables."

The two sisters laughed and proceeded to clean up the mess. As much as Kari loved the hectic environment during operating hours, she looked forward to these small moments closing up shop. This meant that they were finally done for the day, and they could let loose at last.

It was almost as if she was back to the Mills Township she knew, even though it had only been a week since their first encounter with murderers.

Kari and Kasi breathed easier after the Lila Baldwin case was finally put to rest. They were smiling a little bit more, especially Kari. Even their regular customers had noticed the change in demeanor.

Although the sisters had become more vigilant, as anyone in their situation would be, they had stopped constantly looking over their shoulders and had slept considerably better at night. Kari's life was once again peaceful and happy. She's also, hopefully, learned a valuable lesson about thinking before she acted.

Although things had seemingly gone back to normal, Kari was still bothered by the fact that Lila Baldwin, a person who never had a bad word to say to anyone, had her life cut short by people who were only after her aunt's wealth. She thought about the dark power of money, how it could bring out the worst in people and tear families apart. She promised that nothing would ever come between her and Kasi, not even all the money in the world.

If there was something good that came out of this dangerous episode, it was the deeper appreciation of life and the family that came with it.

She also found herself enjoying a newfound closeness to Hunter Houston, and no amount of near-death experiences could bring her down because of that.

She let out a soft smile as the vacuum cleaner sucked up the rest of the glitter powder. Her thoughts had a way of straying too far even as she worked.

If I told my younger self, Kari mused, *that Mills Township would have a murder and that I would encounter the killers in an attempt to solve it, she never would have believed me.*

Kari's adolescent self was a girl who avoided conflicts as much as possible. The adult Kari knew that the younger her would be shocked at the events that occurred last week. Lila's death marked the exact moment when the idyllic neighborhood changed—for Kari, Kasi, and the rest of the town.

A few days before, Lila was laid to rest at the town cemetery. Everyone in town showed up to pay their respects, not that this came as a surprise for both Kari and Kasi.

Lila had always been the kind of person who touched so many lives, regardless of who they were and where they came from. For the residents of Mills Township, Lila was not just a neighbor and boutique owner. She was also a friend.

Flowers of all shapes and sizes enhanced the serene beauty of the service, and the sisters could not help admiring the exquisite arrangement of marigolds, sunflowers, and roses. Kari thought it was a heartwarming and fitting gesture, because Lila had greatly appreciated beauty and loved flowers of every kind.

Lila's aunt, Clementine, who paid for the funeral expenses, greeted the two sisters with much warmth and appreciation. She told them how grateful she was to them for helping the police bring justice for Lila and for trying to protect her from the greedy murderers who kept harassing her. With Lila gone, she thought of Kari and Kasi as her own family.

The sisters returned the favor, too. They made a couple of trips to Behind the Pines to visit not only Clementine, but their landlady Agnes Gaines as well. They promised to visit the two ladies whenever they could, and the pleasure of seeing their happy faces was enough of a reward.

However, there were two people who were understandably upset over the sisters' terrifying ordeal at Behind the Pines: Aaron and Nancy Sweet.

When Kari and Kasi went to visit their parents after the killers' arrest, they received a scolding that felt like it lasted forever. Kari had always thought that her parents were a little protective, but this time, it was on a whole new level. She felt as though she and Kasi went back to being teenagers, admonished all night long for not taking their parents' calls and missing curfew for five nights in a row.

Nancy Sweet, who Kari thought was a pragmatic woman with a progressive mindset, made the sisters promise that they would take self-defense classes. According to their mother, Kari and Kasi were always alone at the coffee shop, and it was best to prepare for the worst.

For Kari, it seemed as though the paranoia of Lila's death would never leave their parents. Natural as it may be for a daughter to feel a little annoyed over nagging parents, she still appreciated the fact that she and Kasi had parents like Aaron and Nancy who were constantly looking out for them.

The family ended up agreeing to invest in self-defense classes, but the two sisters still could not decide if they would go for Krav Maga do or Jiujitsu.

"You ready to go, Kari?" Kasi asked as she turned off the rest of the machinery and wiped off the counter stains.

"Yeah, you go ahead. I have to meet Hunter for dinner tonight."

"Oh, yeah. I forgot. You have another date with your boyfriend. I guess that means more salad and popcorn for me tonight!"

"Shut up, Kasi. He's not my boyfriend."

"Him? The guy who's always asking you out? The guy who always comes in the coffee shop even if he's just gonna order a shot of espresso? I know On Bitter Grounds is the best in town, but I'm pretty sure it's not just coffee he's looking for."

"Whatever."

Kari felt herself blush as she got ready to go out. She was excited to see Hunter again, and she hoped that there would be more dates after this one—preferably with the town safe, peaceful, and murder-free.

"You know, I'm really glad to finally hang out with Hunter without distractions," Kari said.

"What kind of distractions?"

"You know, murder and stuff. I felt a little awkward and out of my element whenever Hunter and I went out during last week's hullabaloo. We always ended up talking about Lila and developments in her case."

"Why wouldn't you appreciate cold-blooded murder as a first date conversation? Don't you wanna spice things up a bit? Wow, you're so boring."

"Maybe you should find your soulmate in crime forums, you little freak," Kari teased.

Outside, the full moon shone luminously above On Bitter Grounds, and the chilly wind coursed through the quiet streets of Mills Township. It was a quiet evening, and all was well.

"Hey, say hi to Hunter for me," Kasi reminded her.

"I will," Kari replied as she exited the doors of the coffee shop.

She and Hunter had agreed to have dinner at a trendy restaurant close to the shop so it wouldn't be much of a hassle for her. Hunter was always considerate of others, especially Kari.

She paused to take in the surroundings before going. Glancing through the shop's windows, she saw her sister still busy with the inventory and some last-minute cleanups.

Much to Kari's amusement, Kasi almost knocked over the shop's candy holders on her way to the broom closet. Kari sighed heavily and smiled.

In Mills Township, everything was fine and dandy.

For now.

Chapter 26

Killer

As Kari Sweet left for her date with Hunter, her sister Kasi was left alone at On Bitter Grounds.

However, she wasn't as alone as she believed herself to be. Inside her coffee shop, Kasi felt safe and secure. That wouldn't have been the case if she had known the truth.

If only Kasi had known that there was a killer watching her…

The killer stood at a distance, waiting for Kari to leave with Hunter, leaving Kasi all alone. Once Kari was gone, they felt emboldened and walked closer to the coffee shop to get a better look at Kasi.

The killer got as close to the window as they thought was safe without being spotted, of course. That would have ruined the plan, and this was a plan that had to go perfectly.

Timing was going to be everything, and right now, it simply wasn't the right time. The idiots who had killed Lila Baldwin had ruined everything for them. Their bumbling in the murder of the clothing boutique owner had turned the world of Mills Township upside down.

"Things would die down, though," the killer told themselves. "Patience is key…and, of course, right timing."

The shadowy figure watched Kasi roasting beans that evening, as it was something she often did alone. That meant the opportunity could present itself soon enough.

This was all the killer could think about. She was all they wanted. The plan was simple, but it was perfect.

Kari often left Kasi alone. The killer knew that. They had done their research.

The killer had been watching the Sweet sisters for a while. Through it all, a plan had developed. It was Kasi who stayed after hours, getting deliveries ready to be picked up.

The killer had observed the sisters' routine countless times, and yet, nobody had ever felt the presence of something sinister. Kasi had no idea what was going on.

She would, soon enough, though. The killer could feel that the time was drawing near.

Nobody was going to get in the way; nobody was going to prevent them from getting what they wanted—and that included Kasi's sister, Kari, and her new boyfriend, the cop.

The killer wasn't going to be denied. There wasn't a person in town that could stop what was coming.

The killer approached the glass of the window carefully, so as not to be seen. They had come too far, and they couldn't risk having everything fall apart at this point.

Kasi had her back to the window. The killer approached it slowly, touching the glass.

"Soon, my beautiful barista…very soon."

And with that, the individual disappeared into the shadows, at least for now.

Thank you for reading!